THE
QUEST

A NOVELETTE

WADE B. FLEETWOOD

A NAMY BOOK

first printing

ISBN:0-9631466-2-9

Library of Congress Catalog

Card Number: 92-97503

Printed in the United States of America

Camera–ready Copy
for this book
Prepared by:

S.A.I.D., inc. and Quick Copy
Falls Church, Virginia

The Cover

Author's concept
by

VALIANT ART SERVICES, INC.
Falls Church, Virginia

For My Five Daughters

Debbye
Tara
Marta
Sandra
Linny

My Five Granddaughters

Shannon
Julia
Lindsay
Jessica
Jordan

My Three Grandsons

Justin Wade
Jared
Terry Travis

and

My Sister

Lou McCutchen of Boise, Idaho

The Author's Notes

Yes, my readers are also writers...of letters:

ETHEL BARRETT, ARCADIA, CALIFORNIA:

"Hurray for you! I don't care how long you take for a new book. The wait is worth it!"

**CAROL DELASKO, CENTRAL CITY,
PENNSYLVANIA:**

"I was the 'fan' who borrowed one of your books and typed the whole book so that I would have a copy for my set."

MICHAEL BUSSACCA, BALTIMORE, MARYLAND

"Again, thanks for the memories."

MRS. EDYTHE N. DODDS, TWIN FALLS, IDAHO:

"I hope you continue to write, always including historical events or special places. Those we haven't visited were made so inviting that we hope to see them some day."

BARBARA J. MILLER, HADDONFIELD, NEW JERSEY:

"Thank you for your invitation to order your latest book. On a snowy winter day, it was like a ray of sunshine."

ELLEN WADLEY ROPER, WASHINGTON, D.C.:

"I've already become an ardent Fleetwood fan. 'The Ghost on Errett Road' made my spine tingle and held my attention every second, as did 'Murder on the Boardwalk.'"

ONE

"A dead man's hand," Clay Stevenson said to the others in the early morning hours, his rapt attention fixed on the hand he held very near his eyes under the bright light.

"Let's see it!" one said, demandingly.

"Very well, gentlemen," and he spread the fanned-card hand on the green felt-covered table with a flourish. "Aces over...read 'em and weep!" He hated that banality but decided there was a need to use it in that instance.

"Well, I'll be damned!" Roger Thomas said. "A lousy two pairs...aces and eights!"

"'Lousy,' yes," Clay said as he used both hands to pull the blue and red chips and assorted high denomination currency toward his place at the table, "but enough, obviously, to win this, shall I say, sizeable pot?" He quickly glanced around at the other faces, none as stormy as Rog's. Some seemed resigned that they were bested; those who folded early, just grinned.

"Two lousy pairs," Rog now repeated. "Hell, I threw away three deuces!"

"Not too astute, Rog," Clay said. "I would have gladly exchanged hands with you." He turned the dagger in the wound. Clay then separated out the bills and placed them neatly behind his stacked colored chips. "Even a dead man, it seems, can win at this game."

"So true," said another player, his discarded hand strewn in front of him. He sipped the last liquid from his can of beer.

"You played them as though you had a pat flush," Rog continued.

"That's part of the game...body language," Clay responded and he lightly touched the pile of bills to make the point.

"My Aunt Tilda!" Rog said as he stood up abruptly and scooted back his chair. "It's past 2 o'clock...I'm beat...Don't count on my vote to extend the time limit. Screw it! I'm going home." Roger then reached across the table and silently shook hands all around and was out the front door.

Slowly, some of the others began to stack and count their chips to cash in with Clay, the banker, who hosted the evening's get-together.

"With Rog's peevish temper showing at times, I don't know if I'd ever want to go under his knife," Jared Marlow said. "I'm afraid he'd cut something he shouldn't."

"Don't you believe it, Jared," Clay said. "When Rog is in that operating room, he's one cool genius. I'd climb up on that table any day and let him slice away. That scalpel is guided by a hand and mind much more skilled than any five-card draw poker hand is ever played. He really hates cards; he loves being a doctor."

"Eighty bucks for me," Justin Wright said as he pushed his chips toward Clay.

"Here are four Jacksons."

"$1,250 for me, Clay." It was Travis Goodson.

"You had a pretty good night, Travis."

When all the tallied chips were in the round, revolving leather holder and the teak bank box was empty, Clay had pocketed nearly $4,000.

"Poor Roger, a big loser again," Travis said as he and the others thanked Clay for a good game and eats and left.

Clay first met Rog at a meeting of the Middlesex Beach Association. It was the annual spring meeting. There was a general hum of conversation in the cavernous room as members all waited in those folding steel chairs at the Bethany Beach, Delaware, Volunteer Fire Company for eleven o'clock to arrive, along with late stragglers.

Clay's mental clock, for years, had always prompted him to get to any meeting, appointment or rendezvous ahead of time and wait. It was far better that way than to walk in late. Those who did, to him, would always be stragglers and poor planners. But, what about an unavoidable delay? To his way of thinking, he always left early enough in case of such a delay and thought others should, too. Plan ahead. If a meeting was worth going to, it was worth getting there on time, at the very least.

The President, at exactly eleven, called the home owners to order for the reading of the minutes of the fall meeting. Just as the secretary rose, minutes in hand, a tall, gray-haired man opened the heavy, side door and quickly took a seat in the back. As he sat down, the door banged shut, of course. A straggler.

Well, that was Rog. At the end of the meeting after twelve, Rog hung around at the back of the room talking with a man on his right, still seated. Clay reached the door to leave at about the same time as Rog, and, since Rog was a stranger to him, Clay introduced himself and shook hands.

"Hi! I'm Roger Thomas."

"Good to know you, Roger. What road are you on?"

"Evergreen. Just bought a place last October."

"I'm on Short. Guess I was among the first in the development. An oldtimer!"

"My wife and kids love the ocean. We're going to like Middlesex."

"Nice to meet you, Roger. Stop by when you're on Short. #21."

"Thanks, Clay."

Rog seemed like a nice guy, even though he was a straggler.

As Clay was about to get into his car out in the lot, Travis, who had parked right by him, started to pull away. He rolled down his window.

"How you doin', Clay? Guess I didn't see you in there. I sat up front for a change," he said.

"Hi, Travis!"

"Say, are you going to be down next weekend?"

"Yeah! I'm planning on doing some painting. Screen doors."

"Good! I'm having a little poker party Friday night. Can you make it?"

"Sure!"

"I'll probably have six guys, all from Middlesex."

"What time?"

"Come on over around eight," Travis said, and drove away.

"Thanks! See you," Clay called out to him.

The sky was blue and the sun was warm. How good to see the end of winter and feel and smell spring in the air again.

Well, that spring those three – Clay, Travis and Rog – were to develop a special relationship as home owners at the beach. But, who among them, by the wildest stretch of the imagination, could have predicted that, before the end of the summer, they would be locked in serious competition for a million dollar prize? Yet that was exactly what was about to happen.

Clay counted Roger and Travis among his closest resort neighbors. He felt more of a spirit of community and friendship with them in Middlesex than he did with people just next door in Georgetown, in Washington, D.C. The reason was obvious: the beach offered recreation, relaxation, an outlet to rejuvenate from the working world; your own hometown neighborhood, on the other hand, was filled with people like yourself, caught up in the routine of schedule, office hours, the traffic hassle every day, shopping and general frustrations that build up in daily living. Most Americans these days sought more leisure and vacation time away from their homes.

Happily, even though the beaches were more crowded than they used to be, what with high-rises and bayside townhouses and new single unit communities like Middlesex, there was still elbow room at this one bright spot of Mother Nature's vast outdoors. It all seemed to balance out in the long run, considering some folks preferred the cool mountains in summertime instead of the beach scene. But, in the years ahead, more and more people would seek a place by the water, too.

So, as he sat down at the poker table that weekend, waiting for all to arrive, Clay felt at home among friends.

Travis, Monty Bell from Addy Road, Jared Marlow and Justin Wright from Evergreen, and Clay from Short all had a bottle of Bud or Coors Light and were at the table, counted chips and made change.

"Who is the sixth?" Clay asked.

"Rog," Travis answered.

It was after 8:30 when Rog showed. A straggler, even to a poker game!

Clay didn't remember much about the game that night, except that the plates of snacks, especially the hard salami, that Travis laid out during a break were first-class. And that he lost eighty bucks. Not bad for him. The big winner, they decided, after each of them guardedly checked his wallet and calculated, was Rog, the last to arrive and the first to want to go home.

It was well after midnight. Clay walked out to the driveway to stretch his legs and the other men soon followed. The air was clean, with a hint of new-bloom fragrance. The tallest pine trees were topped with a blanket of bright stars in a black sky. What a night! "Great Caesar!" Clay exclaimed. It was really quite warm for April and the quietness was only broken when Rog started talking about adding another porch to his house and staining it before rental season.

Travis and Clay had been that route before. They had done all that. Not that beach house maintenance wasn't a full-time extra job, but they had been through the Harry Homeowner's phase years earlier and were glad much of that was behind them. And yet, they knew exactly how Rog felt then. It wouldn't be too long, however, before he reached their level of beach house experience and understanding and, like them, have a little more time to enjoy it. It was still with some wonderment that Clay came to appreciate his own evolution there. It just gradually happened.

Friday wasn't just any day. To Clay, it was a very special day when he was on the way to the beach. That was the best day of the week, at least in those certain weeks. For, when he headed out from Metropolitan Washington, D.C., he knew he would have Friday night, all day Saturday and Saturday night, and one more early stroll at water's edge before heading back on Sunday morning. A weekend could be a perfect mini-vacation at a sanctum of peace at the beach. And he hadn't discovered anything new about "getting away," for hundreds, yes, thousands of folks did the very same thing.

As a self-styled escape artist, Clay well-knew that the practice could become habit forming. He was hooked. But, so be it. The only known cure was to move to...Kansas. If he did, though, he'd be out there in a week or less at that lake or river front, just walking along, pretending it was the Atlantic.

Or, the Pacific. He'd tried that, too, and liked it. There was something about the magic of water —

East or West, North or South – that had a magnet-like tug at human beings. Clay was just proud and happy he was among those attracted to the miracle of rushing, shimmering, lapping or crashing water.

Some day, perhaps in the near future, he planned to make the attraction permanent. Then, rather than longing for the shore, he'd become a fixture there, immovable. He had the beach house and he should use it more than he did. In the meantime, a commuter he must remain.

Monty made some crack a bit earlier about the diamond flush that Travis had been so proud of and had raised to the limit, but lost the pot and, then, he jumped into his new Jeep.

"Next time!" Travis yelled to him, as Monty drove away.

"That's a hell of a good beach car," Rog said.

"Bet it could outrun your T-Bird," Justin threw at Clay. "But, I know, you like a little more car wrapped around you than just a Jeep!"

"Well, gentlemen, with that, it's time I got into that bird and took myself home. Nite, guys."

Clay slipped into the gleaming, classic Thunderbird and started down the road and Jared, the jogger in the group, headed out on his way to Evergreen. Roger and Justin turned toward Evergreen, too, in a slow walk to enjoy the night air and the glory of all the bright stars.

Before the end of June, as beach house owners who rented, came into the prime rental months of the season, the individual members of this particular poker club got a surprise phone call from "Win" Agar. There were other known, regular games all over the area, but this Middlesex Club got the calls.

"Clay, this is 'Win' Agar calling. About got your house in shape for tenants?"

"Hi, 'Win.' Just about."

"Well, good. Clay, I'm hoping you can come to my house for some poker Saturday night."

"This Saturday?"

"Yes. I know it's sort of short notice but it may be my last chance to get you fellows over here before you all have to vacate your places for the summer bunch."

"Yes, I can make it."

"Fine! I've already talked with Monty and Justin can't make it. I'll get ahold of the others this afternoon. Rog was still in Baltimore and Travis was away. But, I'll get 'em all."

"Okay. What time on Saturday?"

"Make it around seven and we'll have a little buffet first."

"Thanks," and Clay hung up, a little taken aback by having "Win" on the other end of the line.

Winfield Agar. Winfield Randolph Agar. Clay first met him when he bought his then-leased lot at Middlesex Beach. For Agar was the joint-owner of the sixty-eight acre tract of land that became the Middlesex Beach community in which Clay built his salt-box beach house. He had met him socially a few

times after that, at cocktail parties or on the golf
course, in beach crowd circles. Everyone called him
"Win," at his insistence, but the name itself, Winfield
Randolph Agar, was, indeed, an impressive one in
business circles and Agar was well-known on the
East Coast. He was a huge man in physical stature,
domineering, but not overpowering, seventy-ish and
still going strong.

Clay had never been inside "Win"'s oceanside
house in Delaware. It took up two lots, with near-
empty lots on either side. He had built a putting
green on one of them; the other held small, grounds-
keeping buildings and, near the dune, a gazebo. The
property was north of Bethany Beach.

A Philippine houseboy, in a white jacket and
black trousers, led Clay from the front door, through
the foyer to a game room off the family room, with
windows overlooking the ocean. The pool table dom-
inated the rear of the room, while black leather sofas
and chairs, placed by massive end and coffee tables,
near the fireplace, balanced the mannishly decorated room. The green felt-covered playing table,
with six identical chairs, was centered toward the
room's windows and a ceiling light lowered to just
above the carved-legged hexagon. Near the French
doors, opening onto the deck, was a lavish buffet,
with the low flames of chafing dishes that flickered

in the light ocean breezes that came through the doors and windows.

Monty and Jared were already there, seated, with cocktails in hand, in comfortable chairs. "Win" stepped forward to greet Clay.

"Clay, I don't believe you have met my wife, Jamie."

Jamie moved from the doorway of the family room and extended her hand to Clay. Clay knew she left her hand in his an extra moment.

"Clay Stevenson, this is Jamie," beamed "Win."

Jamie Agar was the new, young, extremely attractive bride. Clay had only seen her picture in the Wilmington <u>News-Journal</u> last fall, taken at a benefit recital. She was gorgeous closeup.

Travis arrived just then and followed on the heels of Juan, the houseboy.

Lastly, some twenty minutes later, was Rog.

After cocktails, which Juan refilled a couple of times, and quiet chatting among the hosts and their guests, Jamie encouraged all of them to enjoy the buffet.

"Be sure and try the salmon mousse," she said, bade them goodnight and left the room.

"Say, Clay," "Win" said, "do you happen to know an older man in Middlesex Beach by name of Morris, Brad, yes,...Brad Morris, I believe?"

"Heard the name now and again but never set eyes on him. A private investigator, I've heard. But, no, I don't know him."

"Don't know him," Rog added.

"Fine old gent, I'm told. A writer of sorts. Oh, well...just wanted to ask," "Win" said. "I only recently learned he lived around here. Well, let's get to the buffet."

The playing table didn't look like the end of a normal poker game. Juan was too efficient. There were no overflowing ashtrays or empty beer cans in sight. It had been, in that respect, an unusual evening of poker for the Middlesex Beach Club. While neat, it had still been an enjoyable game for the six men. No one had suffered in the surroundings, least of all Clay, who had won $500. "Win" admitted to have dropped quite a few, as had Rog and Monty. Jared was about even and Travis was slightly ahead at the end.

They moved from the table to the more comfortable chairs and Juan offered brandy and coffee.

"Fellas, we had a lot of fun tonight. Now, I want to get right to the point of this get-together, other than the poker, of course," "Win" said with a smile. "I'm about to undertake a large and rather complex business venture with some colleagues. The details of the whole thing are still being developed but I can tell you that I'm in the market for some unorthodox research by level-headed, bright men such as yourselves. You know I could hire all the professionals I need but, for this project, that just isn't what I'm looking for in this thing. I can tell you this: I'm looking for new products and ideas that smack of excellence in this highly competitive business world today. I know that's one hell of an order, but I'm prepared to pay a premium price to the man who can do the most to get this business venture off on the right track."

"But, why us?" Clay asked.

"Because you're all here in the same general area of the country, for starters. My business group is here, too. And, secondly, I already know all your backgrounds and particular talents and I just have a gut feeling that those of you who want to get into this thing may come up with some solid answers I need, and need rather quickly. Lastly, hell, you're all competitors, in a sense, in your professions, maybe with each other and, even right down to a good old poker game. That's why I think I'll get some takers from among you on this quest, if you can call it that."

Clay asked, "Why do you think that we can accomplish something that dozens, hundreds, thousands of trade missions all over the world attempt?"

"Because members of city, state or federal trade missions abroad are not being paid $1 million for something very special. They are seeking more conventional goals, joint ventures, oil exploration, industry infusion, both large and small, in countries seeking jobs and markets and financial assistance. Your task is more specific and not confined to business enterprises. You seek the ultimate: items more out of the ordinary," "Win" answered.

"What is the time frame?" Rog asked.

"By the end of September, at the latest."

"It seems rather vague," said Travis, "about what we'd be looking for out there."

"That's just the point," "Win" answered. "Let me simplify the thing this way: I'm sure you remember as junior high school kids, and even high school, the big thing at those early social parties was the treasure hunt. Remember? Kids at those parties would be divided into three or four teams, each getting an identical list of outlandish, unusual items to collect and bring back to the starting place.

"On the list, were things like a hairbrush with an engraved initial, an Al Jolson record, a cigar, a can of black olives, a right hand glove, a bra, a bowl of oatmeal, a ticket to a play, etc.

"And there was a time limit. Maybe an hour or two. It gave all the guys and gals a chance to pair up and walk down the dark streets, holding hands, maybe, and laugh and have a hell of a time going to doors and asking for the stuff. The team that brought back the most items on the list, won a prize. And, then, they'd all sit around telling how they raised Cain in the neighborhood, what some of the people would say at their doors, and show all the junk they got, while everyone laughed and drank hot chocolate."

"Your telling that brought it all back as clear as a bell. I remember well," Clay said.

"I propose a quest for excellence," "Win" said, "in which there will be no list. Each man who chooses to participate in this thing will be charged with bringing back four items of his choice. That means an object, an idea, an account of an unusual happening and, I would add, a remembrance of an unusual person. In general, I'm looking for something unique, different. Think of it as a search for something we can share and appreciate and evaluate as being outstanding."

"I don't see," Rog said, "how an account of a happening or, for that matter, an unusual person would be marketable."

"Who knows," "Win" answered, "one of my people may get an idea for a new play or a movie script."

"As I see it," Clay interjected, "we may not know what we're looking for until we find it."

"Exactly," "Win" said. "Now, let me take it another step or two. Each of you would be allowed to go anywhere, anywhere in the world, in search of these four items. Or, for that matter, you could stay in your hometown or, hell, there in Middlesex Beach. There would be no restrictions whatsoever. Each of you do some traveling in your work, anyway.

"In order to give some time for you to get your houses in order for this undertaking, I'm depositing a million dollars in Baltimore Trust Company on September 1. At the end of thirty days, one of you can claim that money as the prize.

"I'll ask Judge Brooks to give the decision on this thing. Do you all know him? Sumner Brooks, Sr. He sits on the Federal District bench in Wilmington, a hell of a bright guy. I'll ask him to judge the lists of four. We'll all get together then to hear what he decides.

"But, let me make this clear. The list that each of you may come up with must be in my hands by midnight September 30. That is the absolute deadline. All items and ideas will become my property then.

"Now, one last thing. I'm asking each of you who decides to participate to donate, before September 1, a check for $2,000 to the Bethany Beach Volunteer Fire Company. We'll just call it 'earnest' money."

"How will you know who has decided to go with this thing?" Jared asked.

"Send your checks to John Evans, who lives down here year-round, and was your former resident manager in Middlesex. He's been a volunteer fireman for a long time and he'll let me know on September 1 who's in."

"For your purposes, 'Win,' I guess the more of us who get in, the larger will be the return on your investment," Clay said.

"That's right. Brooks will look at each man's contribution in totality to judge the winner, but all contributions, on all the lists, may have merit for the business venture I've discussed."

"Win" figured he had set it all out to his satisfaction. He thought he had convinced them of the urgency of the matter, from his viewpoint, to the end that they would give his proposal prompt and serious consideration. Though he had no idea what the individual men were thinking, he could see from their expressions during the conversation that each was intrigued by the concept.

For his part, Clay almost smiled to himself as he thought how, over the years, he had debated and fretted about getting a new pump or water conditioner or rug for the upstairs at the beach house and, now, how he was suddenly confronted with the possibility of putting up two thousand dollars on a gamble, just a gamble! Just buying a chance to compete.

Rog, Clay thought, was probably mind wrestling, too. He was thinking about a porch. Today, that ain't cheap. And he had just plunked down some big dough for his house a few months earlier.

In all the faces around the room, you could almost see the wheels turn, each of them looked at and listened to the others as eyes danced in thoughts of objects, ideas, happenings or people that could be exposed at the end of the hunt. There was a strange feeling, too, in the room, as each man reflected in the course of the discussion, that a majority, if not all, were ready, even then, to commit.

But, a commitment and a final plunge into the quest was really not expected until late summer. No one seemed ready, certainly not that night, to declare himself. And, besides, that would be part of the suspense: to wait as long as possible to see if, indeed, such a scheme would come to fruition or not, with players to carry it out.

Clay watched the others and wondered, as each may have wondered, if such a gamble wasn't too rich for his blood, that he was out of his league or that, damn it, the stakes were just too high. It was like putting a big income tax refund check on the line. Or, for that matter, a good part of a season's rentals. Could any of them really afford to do it? Should they?

One way of looking at it was as an investment, a very happy and fortuitous investment, if and when the dividends materialized at the end of September. And, he knew the market would remain bullish. Guaranteed! The dividends would be in a Baltimore Trust Company account, just waiting. How many investments in the stock market caused a man to think of them as "happy" or sound investments, and with the surety of such high, short-term profit? He couldn't think of a single one, blue chips included.

This gamble seemed to have a genuine ring of rightness about it. This investment would, as sure as night follows day, pay off if one's adeptness was right. But, just the decision to participate would be a challenge.

Clay drove home to his beach house and didn't sleep a damn wink the rest of the night. He just stared, in the dark, at the blackish ceiling thinking about the proposal. What in hell happened to last night's poker game and fun and his sleep? It all took second place to the whole, fantastic, all-consuming scheme that came out of "Win"'s head.

Clay tried to focus on his closest friends who had been with him last night. Roger Thomas was a doctor. He could afford this gamble and does get away to travel. Travis Goodson was a lawyer and a good one in a large Washington, D.C. firm specializing in patent and copyright law. He could afford it and often traveled abroad on cases involving international law. And, too, Monty, Jared and, even Justin, had he been at the poker session, were all men of means, in one business or another, and could afford a once in a lifetime really big gamble.

And Clay? A public servant, a "working" bureaucrat, in the executive branch of the federal government could afford it, too.

It wasn't until late July that Clay heard the good news: a series of business meetings were scheduled for Hong Kong, starting September 2, requiring him to visit, after the conference, several embassies in the Far East and Europe. He knew when he put down the phone, that a trip around the world couldn't have come at a better time in his life. It would certainly offer some "on his own time" hours to get seriously involved in the quest.

Before he knew it, it was near the end of August. He had people renting in his beach house through Labor Day and so he wouldn't be going to the beach for a visit until after his trip to Hong Kong and other points on the far side of the globe. And, then, it would be very near the end of September.

He called John Evans from his Washington office on the 26th of August. John told him that Travis had sent him a check for $2,000 on the 24th. So Travis was in! He would be a tough competitor. Clay was curious about who else in the group had put up a check, but was told that Travis' was the only one so far.

On the morning of the 27th, Saturday, Clay called John again and he had Rog's check, too. Clay went to the bank and sent a cashier's check by FedEx. He was in now and thought: right here and now was where we separate the men from the boys. He was in the fray and would undertake the challenge, and the consequences, of the great hunt, no, the great quest.

The next day, soon after he got back to his office from a meeting, his secretary buzzed him on the intercom to say that he had a call waiting, but that the caller wouldn't give her name. Clay said he'd take it.

"Hello, this is Clay Stevenson."

"Clay, this is Jamie."

"Jamie..."

"Jamie Agar."

"Jamie! How are you?"

"Fine. I have a message from 'Win'."

"Okay."

"Not on the phone. I want to see you."

"Where are you? At the beach?"

"I'm at the Mayflower Hotel in Washington. Can you come by the lobby for a drink after five?"

"Sure, I can make it. I'll see you there."

"Bye."

Jamie was in the lobby lounge when Clay arrived. She hadn't ordered.

"What do you like to drink at 5:30 in the afternoon, Jamie?"

"White wine, thank you."

Clay ordered the wine and a scotch and water. Their table overlooked Connecticut Avenue.

Jamie was more beautiful than when he had first met her. She was particularly chic that afternoon.

"I hope you didn't come all the way to Washington just to deliver the message," Clay said. "If you did, it must be mighty important."

"No, I drove over this morning to do some shopping. And, forgive me, there is no message. I just wanted to get to know you better."

Clay sipped his drink and swirled the ice cubes with the stirrer.

"'Win' is in Rome and I wanted to get away from the beach crowds for a few days. Besides, I love the shops here, especially those in Georgetown."

"Well," said Clay, "I'm flattered by your attention."

"Are you married, Clay?"

"I was. My wife died very young, years ago."

"Why have you never remarried? I know it's none of my business, however, and you needn't answer."

"I don't mind in the least. After the death long ago, I got deeply involved in my work and traveled a great deal. And I figure on retiring from government before long and trying my hand at writing. Guess I have a lot I want to try and say."

"Are you going to take 'Win' up on his proposal?"

"Yes, I am. You remember Travis and Rog? They are, too. Fifty percent out of the club, so far, is pretty good, don't you think?"

"It's wonderful. Not to change the subject but I took the liberty of buying you a small gift at the jewelry store off the lobby. It is for your birthday."

"How did you know? I'll be half way around the world on that day."

"We Agars know almost all about you, remember?"

"It was very thoughtful of you."

They talked for another half an hour or so. Clay brought her up to date on his trip and showed his excitement about the quest.

Clay thought of Jamie Agar for a time. He was attracted to her all right, as she, to him. She reminded him a great deal of his young bride of twenty years earlier and his loss of her after a scant year of marriage. Jamie suspected that Clay was thinking then of his late wife by his quick glances at her.

"Do you want to talk about it?"

"Oh, of course," Clay answered. "It was all so long ago. I was just out of Georgetown University in this city where I took the State Department's foreign service exam." He spoke low and seriously.

He explained that he passed the grueling, yet compressed, written test at the top of all of the regional candidates' scores and took and passed the oral exam, in stride, by his knowledge of world affairs, literature, his fluent French and international and national politics in general. He didn't wait long for an assignment: he worked for a time in the office of the Undersecretary of State and even more briefly at the U.S. Embassy in Saigon before returning to Washington near the end of the war.

It was rather jokingly said by insiders at State, Clay related, that you had it made if your pants' cuffs had picked up lint from the blue carpeting on the 7th and 8th floors near the office of the Secretary of State. That, and a parking space in the mammoth garage under the "New State" building were the badges worn by those who had managed to climb the bureaucratic rungs upward. Of course, if one had suffered no free-falls from grace or during changes of political administrations from one party to the other, you were a consummate professional, an untouchable. And it wasn't all that easy for everyone. The hallways in the Department of State, at 23rd Street and Virginia Avenue, N.W., as well as many of the department's annexes, were known to have Ph.D's working as mailmen pushing mail carts from office to office, patiently waiting for assignments more in line with their educational backgrounds. It all was indicative of the strong desire and passion to serve in the Department in some role, somewhere, anywhere around the globe, in an official capacity, on behalf of the government of the United States. Your résumé certainly required a "posted" or country assignment to commence to carry any weight in the bureaucracy that abounded in the nation's capital.

In those early days at State, Clay met a comely Argentine, a consular officer, Thomasina, or Tommi, as he called her, and they married. When she was assigned to Africa early in the marriage, Clay sought and undertook a dismal, hardship post in Chad and soon learned from hard experience the challenges of being out of the States in an impoverished nation deep in the heart of north Central Africa. Fort-Lamy, the capital, a former French possession in days gone by, brought his French into play, as it had in Vietnam, and was one of the reasons he was selected for the post. Of Tommi, he told Jamie, she was struck down in Chad by the Ebola virus, a hemorrhagic virus with high fever, liver problems and both internal and external bleeding. The virus had been identified in the mid-1970's by the Antwerp Institute of Tropical Medicine. Tommi lingered but days in a ravishing fever and complications before she could be medevacked out to more modern hospital facilities. It was too late.

Clay said he had been deeply touched when she wrote to him in earlier days that he was the biggest plus in her life; and, to Clay, she was, in his. One letter contained these lines:

All life like a fabric is woven
And textured by things we do
Our dreams, our duties make patterns
Each day we start weaving anew

"What marvelous words she wrote," Jamie said.

Clay told her, too, that he was stunned by the sudden, personal tragedy and he shunned serious romantic liaisons and became a confirmed bachelor, immersed in his work with the Department. He won new assignment out of Africa and quickly ascended the ladder of bureaucratic power and served brilliantly in Rio and Paris before rotation back to the States.

"And so, Jamie, that brings things up to date."

"Thanks for sharing with me."

TWO

From his first look at Dulles International Airport years ago, Clay always thought of it as some futuristic creation on the moon. The oversized control tower and the sweeping, graceful tilt of the terminal's gigantic roof were enough to give him that impression. When first seen at night, as he drove along the rolling, Virginia hills and the predominate structures, blazing with lights, came into view on the horizon, he wondered if he had approached by rocket. Sitting on such a vast, isolated tract of land, the size of the airport facility alone was a compelling argument to him for transferring more traffic from crowded Washington National. And it was, but Dulles had recently been enlarged, as had National, even more.

Once inside, Clay was struck by the great height of the floor to ceiling windows on the front side of the building and the pragmatic physical arrangement of ticket counters and services. Even the modernistic chairs in the waiting areas by the gates and, especially, the transport vehicles to planes, helped carry out the theme of the future of flight. The whole, immense scene at Dulles still took his breath before he even boarded a plane and left the ground.

He went to a pay phone and called John at the beach. He confirmed that he had received the check for $2000, Clay's earnest money.

"Listen," John said, "the boys at the firehouse are going to be mighty happy with the six grand. I'm taking the checks to them this morning."

"John, tell 'em for me it's my pleasure."

"Have a great trip and happy hunting", he shouted.

Clay hung up the receiver and paused just long enough for it all to sink in. He quickly thought that Rog, Travis and he were only hours away from the start of one of the biggest challenges they'd ever faced. All he could think was, may the best man, yes, may the man with the best imagination, win.

Clay walked over and sat down in a chair. He knew his life wouldn't be the same for at least thirty days. This was not only a special business trip to Hong Kong, but one that would take him on his first trip around the world. That, in itself, made the venture exciting. But, now, added to it, was the fact

that he was going to be on a very demanding quest
that would take every ounce of his inner resources.
He knew he had to reach into his past experiences
for guidance and that all his senses would have to
be razor honed. He would have to be his own evalu-
ator, judge and analyst on this trip as he began his
search for those four items for his list. Oh, he was
very sure of one thing: this wasn't just another trip.
Hell, he had been on dozens of trips in his work over
the years, but this trip required that he call up all
his energy to enable him to succeed not only on the
business side but, also, in undertaking the extra job
of searching for excellence to satisfy "Win"s conditions.

He knew even then, as he sat, that he was
already a changed man. The routine of his former
travel had been transformed now into an exact science, practically, to cope with the needs and demands of the hunt. He would henceforth have to be
extremely alert to ideas, words, acts, people and,
especially, his own interpretations of what was going
on around him. The most subtle thing might just
turn out to be what he was looking for. He simply
had to turn on his radar if he expected to be a serious
competitor and his actions, reactions and general
intelligence would be tested to the limit if he expected to win this game. He now knew that anything
and everything could have a bearing on the final
outcome. He couldn't waste any time in the precious
thirty days allotted to him.

They soon called his flight for boarding. He had
flipped the pages of a Time magazine, barely seeing

the words and pictures on the pages, as he sat in front of Gate 12. There was a full load of passengers going to the West coast and, after his ticket was checked again by the agent, got seated in the mobile unit for the ride to the plane, parked at a service area.

Later, as the huge plane roared down the runway, the Dulles Terminal building, once so large, now dwindled in size to only an odd-shaped box, Clay thought, sitting off to one side, as they quickly gained altitude. And, then, it was gone from view and the steady hum of jet motors and minor vibration took over part of the passengers' senses inside the plane as they settled down for the cross-country flight.

Clay had tried to sleep, but, less than an hour out, he stirred, shifted in his seat and looked down at fleecy clouds and patches of ground passing by. For some reason, he suddenly remembered reading how President Roosevelt, prior to the end of the Second World War and the founding of the United Nations, had envisioned a majority of the world delegates going by train from the East coast to San Francisco for the conference on the U.N. Charter. His thought was to impress them with the breadth and variety of terrain, between oceans, that made up the continental United States. They would see many of our factories and farms and rivers and great cities and the plains, mountains and deserts, together with small towns and people from all walks of life. A panorama of America, the most powerful nation on

earth, and its people would pass in front of their
eyes.

Now, for Clay, so impersonally, a whole country
slipped by, mostly out of sight. In just less than five
hours from take off, he would leave it all behind.
Most of the world, in fact, that he would see on this
trip, would have to be seen from the ground.

That was the way he saw Moyabamba, in Peru,
in the Andes. It was during a time early in his career
when Clay traveled a great deal in Latin America.

On one of those trips to Peru, Clay and a Peace
Corps representative were to go to Chuchin, north of
Lima in an Andean valley, and then to Moyabamba
to deliver a Little Library, donated by a service club
in Texas. The library consisted of over a hundred
paperbacks in Spanish. And Clay was to get some
pictures of the roof of a school, financed by students
of Jamestown Elementary School in nearby Arlington, Virginia.

They stayed overnight in Chuchin. There was no
electricity or running water in their hotel room, nor
in the entire community. But, the bed sheets on their
cots were neat and just as white as any he'd seen in
the Hiltons and Holiday Inns at home. And the
hand-woven blankets were warm in the high Andes.
A flickering candle illuminated the whitewashed
walls of the room with the neatly swept dirt floor.

At dawn, Clay paced about outside on the unpaved street waiting for the pack train to take them
to Moyabamba. His heart sank a little as he saw two
horsemen and three extra horses descend, in the
early light, from a nearby mountain trail to get

them. One man was the mayor of Moyabamba; the other, his young grandson.

Loading up, the small train of four horsemen and a pack horse, with gunny sacks full of books roped across its back, headed out and up the steep and rocky trail. Gradually, Chuchin would diminish, then disappear from sight, and then, reappear, even smaller by the river. The views became more spectacular with each switch-back on the hand-hacked trail and ancient, terraced Inca walls on adjacent green mountainsides soon loomed and etched their unforgettable patterns of perfect contours on his mind.

Higher up, Clay was handed a straw hat by the mayor and told to put it on to protect his face from the growing intensity of the climbing sun. By now, the river had become a twisted, golden ribbon nestled near Chuchin, far below.

And two hours later, at last, the top and Moyabamba. After a brief respite at the church, the townspeople received the books in a happy ceremony and a local artisan carried a beautiful, hand-carved bookcase into the tiny community building to house the library, their first. And when speeches ended and they had eaten sandwiches and talked with the town's leaders over coffee, the riders made their descent.

Back down in Chuchin, Clay gave the mayor a shiny Kennedy half-dollar and he guessed he had it still. For Clay knew that he would always have his own special memories of the mountain trail and Moyabamba.

Clay walked down the aisle to the lavatory. On the way back, he heard two men nearby laughing and calling out numbers.

"Gimme a six!"

"You'll never get it!"

"Six! I got it!"

"Damn!"

Clay stopped and held onto the backrests, steadying himself in the light turbulence, and asked, "What's the game?"

"Just a little dice game," said the ruddy-faced man in shirtsleeves, his tie loosened and collar unbuttoned. "I don't even think it has a name." He took another sip of his wine and straightened the box on the seat beside him.

"A buddy of mine," said the other, with a bunch of paper dollars in his hand, "pulled this game out at a party once. He just called it 'Cover-up'." Might have originated in Washington, D.C., Clay thought.

"Yeah," said the first man, "but he just made that up. He said he first ran across it in Ethiopia."

"What's the point of it?" Clay asked.

"Well, the idea is to cover up all these numbers from one through nine," said the shirt-sleeved man, who flipped the wooden pieces up, and exposed the nine numbers in the box. "This is a homemade job," he said, as he pointed to the cedar cigar box. "Made it myself!"

Clay looked across at the box on the empty seat between the men. The man had lined it with green felt and, at the back of the box, on the inside, had glued the numbers in a row - 1, 2, 3, etc. to nine.

Above them, on leather hinges, were nine dominoes that, when flipped down, covered one number at a time. That was all there was to it, besides a pair of dice. The man had done a good job with makeshift materials, Clay thought.

"Two or more can play," said the builder. "High dice goes first. Say you roll a nine. You have the option of covering the numbers any way you want, in any combination - like nine, five and four, seven and two, six and three, etc. But, no more than two numbers can be covered at a time. When the seven, eight and nine are covered, you use one die. Then, the player continues to roll, trying to cover all the numbers. If he rolls a number already covered, he passes the dice to the next player, who starts his turn with all the numbers showing again. Whoever covers the board, wins. If no one can cover it all, the player who had the lowest number remaining on the board wins."

"Simple," said the wine drinker.

"Sounds like fun," Clay said, as he started to move away.

"It is and pretty fast. Even with more than two players."

"Nice game," Clay said as he went on down the aisle to his seat.

Clay smiled to think that he'd be traveling so far west on this trip that he'd end up in the Far East. He read, chatted with a neighbor, did some writing and had a scotch and water before lunch to celebrate his start of a trip around the world. He was getting into a really long journey.

The pilot reported that they were over the Grand Canyon. As Clay looked out at the shining rims and the reddish colors below, the pilot added that he had asked LA for permission to make a turn so that all passengers could get an unusually good look. LA said absolutely not; too many aircraft in the area headed for the same spot. Thank goodness, Clay thought, for a cool-headed LA air traffic controller.

Clay was a little taken aback to learn they would have to go to San Francisco before Tokyo. But, that was the pilot's next message for on-going passengers. The only consolation would be to get a look at the Golden Gate Bridge that afternoon. Clay felt that routing him Washington, Los Angeles, San Francisco to Tokyo was ridiculous. Why did they? He would have preferred a polar flight, with a stop in Anchorage, rather than this. Maybe no reservations were available at the time. At least he was on his way to his first extended visit to Asia, but, already, time was being wasted.

He must have slept a bit. When he looked from the window, planes and buildings were racing by, just as the wheels abruptly whined on gentle impact with the runway.

They deplaned and walked into the Los Angeles terminal for the change of planes. He took time to feel the firm ground under his feet at an airport restaurant, where a Chinese waitress told him he could use a quiet table in the back. She said, "You go back there and do your stuff!" He wrote some postcards and started a journal of his trip.

There was another delay for their plane and he ended up waiting for several hours. He walked around aimlessly inside the building and, then, outside in the warm, sunny weather. His growing impatience, however, got him thinking of how much he had always disliked LA and its sprawl and freeways and hassle at the airport. This stop only confirmed his feelings for the place.

Later, he sat, somewhat slouched, to compose a scolding letter in his mind to Pan Am, when his flight was called and he boarded his first 747. It was gigantic, he thought. He was one of about forty who got into the flying boat and, while it held hundreds, the closest people to him were about shouting distance away. There were about ten stewardesses aboard, a very favorable ratio of passengers/service, he thought.

They got off the ground so easily. What power, he almost said aloud. He looked around and felt like one of the last sardines in a can.

It was unbelievable that, after yet another stop, nearly thirteen hours had elapsed since Dulles and that they were just now climbing out of the airport at 8 P.M., San Francisco time, with a full complement of passengers. The pilot told them that it was now noon tomorrow in Tokyo. Over the din, Clay heard him say it would take ten hours and thirty minutes to fly non-stop and they'd arrive at 10:30 p.m. the next night.

The first thing he thought about as the 747 climbed over the obscured Bay was Sir Francis Drake and his ship, "The Golden Hind," that may

have touched what was now that great harbor. That
Englishman, the navigator, had set sail in 1577 and
three years later returned home after circumnavi-
gating the earth. But, the interesting thing to Clay
about Drake and his ship was the brass plate found
thirty miles northwest of the Golden Gate in 1936.
Known as the Drake plate, it was strong evidence
that he had visited the California coast on that trip.
Though still disputed, the plate was a curious find.
Clay had read about it at the Bancroft Library in
Berkeley while doing a Ford Foundation research
project there. Would that he could find such an object
for the quest!

"Sir, would you like a cocktail before dinner?"

Clay didn't hear her. He had closed his eyes and
was at the Sir Francis Drake Hotel in San Francisco.
He had stayed there on his last visit and was at the
bar in Drake's Tavern. What a delightful place, he
thought, after riding the Hyde and Powell Street line
cable car to Fisherman's Wharf. The little cable cars,
to Clay, made up a not-so-small part of San
Francisco's lasting charm. He loved them, even if the
one he rode that day nearly took him and a couple
dozen others on a roller-coaster ride at Washington
and Mason Streets. That was where the cable-grab-
ber mechanism failed. Happily, they were at a level
intersection and the car stopped before teetering
forward.

"Sir?"

Clay opened his eyes and jumped forward a
little. The couple next to him stifled their laughing
at their startled seatmate.

"I'm sorry," Clay said, "I must have dropped off. Thank goodness it wasn't the cable car!"

"I'm Bruce Tipton and this is my wife, Anne. We couldn't help but laugh a bit when you woke up."

"Hi! I'm Clay Stevenson. Don't apologize! I think I need a scotch!"

"Rocks?" asked the stewardess.

"Please, with some water. May I buy the Tiptons a drink?"

"Two scotch and waters, too, for us." Bruce said. "Thank you, Mr. Stevenson."

"Clay!"

"Clay. What was that about the cable car?"

"Oh, that. I was just thinking about my last visit to San Francisco, a broken cable car and, well, I must have dozed a second."

"On business to Tokyo?"

"Hong Kong. What about you?"

"Tokyo."

The drinks were placed on the trays along with bags of macadamia nuts. Bruce and Anne raised their glasses to Clay, his, to them with "salud."

"With the government?" Bruce asked.

"State Department."

"Well, two government types, off to splendidly represent their country abroad! I'm with the Patent Office."

"Really? Like me, you probably get a lot of 'Do you know so and so? He works there, too!' questions. But, a friend of mine at the beach is a patent attorney in D.C. Name is Travis Goodson."

"Travis? Hell, yes, I know him!"

"Small world!" said Anne.

"I've worked with Travis on a few cases in the last few years. Keeps inviting Anne and me to the beach. Delaware, isn't it? We've got to take him up on it one of these times."

"I hope you do. Bethany's great."

"We usually try to slip down to OC at least once a year, but we like to ski more than do the beach."

"Where do you go?"

"Steamboat Springs mostly. Aspen sometimes. Last year, to Stowe."

"Know Smuggler's Notch?"

"Stayed there!"

"Why don't you two come on down to Hong Kong after Tokyo. We seem to have a lot in common."

"Bruce, why don't we? We've never been and we may never be so close again," Anne said.

"We'll talk about it. I've got the leave."

"You better use some! You know what they say: Use it or lose it!" Anne said with a smile.

Clay's mind was suddenly filled with visions of blurred objects, yet unknown, that he might bring back from the hunt and enter in the all-important judging a month from now. What kind of thing might be outstanding? Unusual? The possibilities, what with going around the world, seemed so limitless. "Win" was wise, indeed, to give them so much leeway, yet it was maddening to think of compressing such a multitude of things down to just four. Adding ideas to objects and an account of a happening or remembrances of people, within the four, made the task almost staggering. To get a list down to the best four was going to be the real challenge.

"Look at Clay," Brandy said, "he's already gone to Hong Kong. He's got a head start on you and you just sit." She was angry, and a little unusual for her to show it. Her life as a doctor's wife had always been slightly immobile, however, dependent upon him being able to get away, first from the confining school years, then internship and, later, the hospital and the clinic.

"Well, damn it, Clay was lucky as hell to get a trip out of the blue. I'm surprised, when you think how slowly the wheels of the damn government turn. He must have put some pressure on someone," Rog said.

"Someone better put some pressure on you or you'll be stuck at the clinic for the whole month. I don't know if Mr. Agar will be interested in a gall bladder!"

"Very funny, Brandy. Very funny."

"Why don't you have some words with that does-as-he-pleases associate of yours and tell him you're leaving for a vacation?"

"I just can't take a month off any time I want to. You should know that by now. We've scheduled some operations. And patients can't wait."

"Well, the chance to put aside part of a million dollars for the kids' education can't wait, either."

"You're pretty confident I'll win! I'm glad the kids' education thing doesn't depend on Judge Brooks. I've heard he's handed down some strange decisions during his tenure."

"Well, darling, I just wanted to get my two cents worth in to let you know that making some priority decisions will be helpful."

Rog got his coat from the hall closet and, looking back at her, went out the front door. He didn't exactly slam it, but shut it firmly, without a word.

At the clinic, the Charge Nurse handed Rog some telephone messages as he headed for his office. The traffic in downtown Baltimore was snarled that morning, too, and didn't help his frame of mind. She saw he was irritated.

"Thanks, Marie," Rog said as he hurried down the corridor. He tossed the phone slips on his desk, took off his coat and put on his white jacket. Sitting down at his desk, he picked up the first telephone slip, dialed and leaned back in his chair.

"Hello," said the voice on the phone.

"John, this is Rog."

"Rog! Thanks for getting back to me."

"What's up?"

"Just wanted you to know that it looks like there will be three of you taking 'Win' up on his offer. I got Clay's check and a call from him at Dulles."

"Great! I knew he was going on a trip and I'm glad he joined us."

"Those donations to the Fire Company are much appreciated."   •

"Thank 'Win', John. It was his idea."

"I just wanted you guys to know we're grateful, even if it was his way of committing you. We'll put it to good use."

"I'm glad. Besides, it's deductible!"

"Thanks for the call, Rog, and good luck."

"Say, John, I didn't want to bug the others to see if they were getting in. They may think I was pushing them. But, you've only heard from Clay, Travis and me, right?"

"That's right."

"Tomorrow is the deadline on earnest money, so I guess we're it."

"If I hear from anyone else, I'll let you know."

"Thanks. I just want to know who the competition is, you know."

"Okay, Rog."

Then Rog dialed Travis in Washington. He told him that John had only heard from them and Clay and that was it.

"Funny Clay didn't give us a call," Travis said.

"I know Clay. He'd rather let the suspense build in our minds as to whether or not he'd put up the money. And, too, he was probably cutting it a little close, what with getting ready for that trip of his."

"I'm sure you're right."

"You have any plans to head out?"

"Ainsley and I are talking about the Panama thing. Figure we may make that our vacation spot and catch a patent convention in Panama City while we're there. It's an Inter-American annual meeting."

"Sounds good. Won't be long till the first of September. Lord, that's tomorrow!"

"I know. And thirty days go like the wind. What about you?"

"I've got to get some help into the clinic so I can get freed up. I'm working on it," Rog said.

Rog put down the phone. So Clay got in! Looked like it would be the Three Musketeers doing battle with the unknown enemy – and maybe with each other! It still didn't sound right to him that Clay didn't call before he left. He'll be a slick competitor, that bastard, Rog thought. I'll bet he's picking the brains already of every passenger on that damn plane and probably making notes. Shrewd guy, for a government employee.

Travis buzzed his secretary.

"Helen, see if you can reach Ainsley at home, will you, please?"

"Yes, Mr. Goodson."

Stuffing some papers into a folder and putting it into his slim leather briefcase, Travis gently snapped it shut and placed it on the floor by the end of his desk.

Then, he swung around in his chair and, gripping a pencil tightly in his fingers, looked out on 15th and G Street, N.W. and watched the end of rush-hour traffic crawl by from ten stories up. It was humid as hell and already eighty degrees out there.

"Mr. Goodson, your wife is on line four," Helen said into the intercom. Travis whirled from the window and picked up the phone.

"Listen, Ainsley, I thought you'd like to know that Clay is in with Rog and me on the 'Win' proposal."

"He'll be tough."

"Hell, I'm tough! So is Roger."

"I know. I just mean that Clay travels quite a bit and it seems to me he's got a big advantage with taxpayers' travel money."

"Look, that's part of his job. Clay doesn't make as much as some of the other professions, either. Ainsley, I've got to be over in District Court in twenty minutes, and I just wanted you to know about Clay in this quick call. Also, I love you."

"Good! I love you, too! When you get home tonight, we'll talk about our trip!"

"Okay. See you!"

"Bye, bye."

The sleek, black limousine waited at the lower level, just off the baggage area, of Dulles International. The driver had the motor running and the air-conditioned car, with its dark-tinted windows, kept the man inside comfortable. A car such as this was so commonplace in Washington that loaded-down passengers exiting the building didn't give it a second glance. If they had, they might have thought it was waiting for a member of Congress just back from the Middle East or Central America, hurrying to the Hill to report on new findings after the August recess.

Though that might often have been the case, the limo's driver quickly got out and opened the trunk when he saw "Win" signal to him from the doorway to the baggage room. He scurried inside the building, spotted his employer and half-ran to pick up the two suitcases, which had been set aside near the baggage conveyor belt.

"How are you, Robert?", "Win" asked him.

"Fine, sir. Pleasant flight?"

"Fine as frog's hair, Robert."

"Good, sir."

"Has the weather been terrible like this while I was away?"

"Just like this, sir. Terrible."

"Win" carried his briefcase and, when Robert opened the rear door at the curb, got into the spacious back seat, loosened his tie a bit and picked up the morning's copy of the <u>Wall Street Journal</u> beside him. Robert slowly pulled away from the terminal and headed down the access road toward the city.

"Take me to the Hart Senate Office Building, Robert," "Win" said, as he shuffled pages to find the futures section of the paper.

The terminal soon far behind, the limo glided swiftly along the Dulles access road, Route 66 and George Washington Parkway, slowed for the exit to the Theodore Roosevelt Island Bridge spanning the Potomac River, then picked up speed again on a

near-straight shot, almost traffic free, down Consti-
tution Avenue to Capitol Hill. It was hours before
rush hour on a black morning, only the signals along
the grand avenue competing with their red, amber
and green against the few headlights of white the
limo encountered.

By both choice and seniority, the latter far the
most important, Senator Blake's office was in the
Hart Senate Office Building, the newest of the three
mammoth structures that held spacious committee
rooms and plush, coveted suites for Senators and
staffs of both.

Earlier, when Clay first saw the interior of the
white marble Hart Senate Office Building, his
thoughts ran to the sumptuous galleria as seen at
the Tyson's Corner II Shopping Mall in Virginia, just
back across the Potomac River. Great Caesar! he
thought: the similarity of the two in both size and
opulence would certainly out-Julius Caesar's Rome
as the glittering gem at the center of an empire in
ages long past. But, as most Americans knew too
well, Senators felt little guilt or pain in their brief,
perfunctory, polite debate and then voted to appropriate many millions and millions in tax dollars to
provide the space, with some views of the Capitol
Dome, they felt were so richly deserved by the select
members of the world's greatest deliberative body.
The Forum of Rome paled when compared to the
exquisite luster of the chamber of the United States
Senate, designed and crafted by world-renowned
artisans from many countries using marble, exotic
woods, plush carpeting, and even goldleaf adorn-

ment on doors, and rich fabric on the walls that highlighted the meeting place for 100 men and women who served there and savored the exalted title of Senator.

"Senator, good to see you," "Win" said.

"How are things in Wilmington, 'Win'?"

"I haven't the slightest idea this week, Senator. I just got in from Rome." Senator Hudson Blake slapped "Win" on the back and ushered him into his office and closed the door.

"Well, how are things in Rome?"

"Still the crazy traffic!"

"What brings you to see me, 'Win'?"

"I just wanted to bring you up to date, Hud, on the business venture I've discussed with you before."

"The one that may require some special legislation?"

"No, the one that may make me, and some silent partners, a little fatter than we are," "Win" said, slightly raising his eyebrows.

"Well, 'Win', as a matter of fact, I have been losing a little weight lately. Even my doctor says I should get a bit more meat on my ribs!"

Both men leaned back in their easy chairs and laughed.

The Senator poured "Win" a bourbon and himself a splash and put the bottle back in the cabinet. And, then they spoke in quiet earnest tones together.

"Hud, according to the last word I heard in Rome, three men have agreed to do some spadework for us in this thing."

"You know them personally?"

"Each of them. Each has his own specific unique talent. I know they are dedicated down to their bones."

"When will you see them next?"

"One has already gone to the Far East and I imagine the other two will get on their way soon after I get back to the beach tomorrow. I'd be back late this afternoon but I'm stopping over at the Carlton to see, ah, a business associate."

"Did you give these men a time limit to report back to you?"

"I set a thirty-day limit, ending on the 30th of this month."

"Can three do the job?"

"Three times as good as one."

"Keep me informed, 'Win'."

THREE

Clay dozed, even in the light turbulence that lasted for over an hour, as the 747 pushed on and, then, sleep got to him. He must have felt safe and comfortable, high over the Pacific.

It was about 11 P.M., San Francisco time, when he awoke. They were only three hours out of the U.S., like Washington, D.C. to Denver in time and miles, still seven and a half hours to go till Tokyo. He noted that the Tiptons slept soundly.

Clay was both an impatient and queasy air traveler. A timid flyer, he was uneasy most of the time in the air. Sometimes he couldn't eat, or didn't, because he worried about rough air spilling his coffee or making him airsick. He usually could hardly wait till the plane landed. Strangely, he felt more safe on take offs and landings, the opposites of the norm.

Once, from Minot, North Dakota, he flew in an Apache to Minneapolis. It was near midnight when they left the ground at Minot, made a few turns and, after climbing to the proper altitude, leveled out. He asked the pilot what he could do to be helpful, as if, he really thought, he could do anything except just sit still. But the pilot rather nonchalantly said, "Watch for any approaching aircraft!"

Before long, up there in the blackness of the sky, as he watched twinkling town lights pass slowly by, the pilot asked him to pour coffee from the large thermos. Clay passed a cup to him successfully, poured his own, capped the thermos and was about to take a sip when they hit violent turbulence. He balanced the cup out in front of him and felt like he was dancing on a stage, but spilled great slops of hot coffee, all the while, on his pants and shoes. After that act, it seemed to take hours to get to Minneapolis.

And the time, out of Las Vegas in a 707, after a thunderstorm, when that huge plane just seemed to drop hundreds of feet several times and he wondered if the wings would catch it.

Or the time he came into Dulles after a non-stop flight from San Francisco. It was a Christmas morning and the plane was loaded with servicemen coming home for the holidays from Vietnam. It was on the descent into the Washington, D.C. area after a great snowstorm and it was like a giant washboard all the way down. And, of course, he heard the comment all around him about the severity of the rough flight, many men saying they had never been in military aircraft in Vietnam that got so shook up.

A Chinese friend in Denver even used to tell him where to sit on a plane. "Never be where the wings can come in on you in a crash - landing," he was told. His friend investigated air tragedies and also told him about metal fatigue. Like, on this long flight to Tokyo, Clay just figured the plane might, somehow, develop that condition going six hundred miles per hour for nearly eleven hours. So far, the plane didn't even seem to need its second wind.

And there were many other times, some in Latin America, that caused him to appreciate the term, "white knuckle flight." His first trip to Bogota was one.

The approach to Bogota required a steep dive over the mountains. Well, in a jet, with clouds, as usual, and rough air, it was a struggle, as were some flights he took into parts of Central America. But, he had to face it: there weren't any trains to those stops!

Once, as he traveled from San Jose to Limon, on the east coast of Costa Rica, he flew in a cargo plane, boxes strapped to the floor in front of a few same-class passenger seats. He remembered the plane had doors, a crew of two and that the flight was rough. Limon's air strip was right next to the beach and the lace-like breakers, coming onto the shore, were especially beautiful. It made the landing easier.

And, now, he was in the midst of another flight, his longest non-stop, and still faced a series of hops country to country, that, prayerfully, would get him back home again.

Home, to Clay, not long ago, was Arlington, Virginia. Few in his old neighborhood could forget their excitement and pride in the achievement of their former neighbor, John Glenn, a man with no fear of being at great heights. Then an astronaut, Glenn lived on the opposite side of Williamsburg Junior High School from Clay. His modest, frame house became a focal point for not only the neighborhood, but also the world press after his successful three-orbital space flight in a Mercury capsule in 1962.

Aside from the White House treatment accorded him by a grateful President Kennedy, who had geared our space program to beat the Russians to the moon, and an address by Glenn before a joint session of the Congress, the old neighborhood had done Glenn honor, too.

The welcoming crowds at his home were kept behind police barricades in the school's parking lot across the street. Clay's film footage on the old Bell and Howell movie camera was carefully spliced to an official film on Glenn's trip, from launch to splashdown, and still evoked vivid memories of a hero's welcome when shown.

But, the personal encounters with Glenn shortly after the flight were the ones that really stood out in memory. Armed with a first day of issue stamp cover and a copy of LIFE magazine which bore Glenn's picture on the cover, Clay went to Glenn's front door. He was ushered into his living room by shirtsleeved Glenn, who autographed the items and shook hands, as a neighbor would. Those framed autographs still hung in Clay's beach house. For John Glenn was Clay's most famous neighbor. At least he was the only one who brought the police, and the crowds, in large numbers.

The plane sped on. A little choppiness was felt now and then over the unseen Pacific. The stewardesses dispensed blankets and pillows to all takers and dimmed the lights in the cabin.

Memories, too, of some of the old days in the Latin America bureau came back into his mind. Let 'em, he thought. He had a lot of time on this long flight. They had seeped in before on this trip, so why try and lock them out now? And the Tiptons still slept.

The only time he ever felt like Lindbergh, or Glenn, was in Pelileo, which was a tiny mountain town in Ecuador a few hours outside Quito. He had gone to Pelileo with his boss to represent the people of Idaho in a celebration that marked the inauguration of a new partnership of peoples, north and south.

They drove the high, rocky roads one morning to reach Pelileo and were startled to find that the whole town awaited their arrival. In fact, the parade through the unpaved streets was about to begin. They hastily took their places in the procession and an unforgettable day in his life began, for they led the dignitaries of the community through the cheering, waving crowds.

The clergy, the mayor, the other local officials, together with representatives of the governments of

Ecuador and the U.S., all fell into line as they slowly walked the few short blocks to the community building. But, to Clay, it was New York's City Hall. School children and townspeople and others, probably from miles away, jammed the parade route, waved flags and showed bright smiles.

Our returned former prisoners of war or our American hostages from Iran, and, yes, even the Super Bowl Washington Redskins' championship team, knew no welcome as that day in Pelileo seemed to him. And, to the people of the town, it meant that, perhaps for the first time, the outside world had reached out to them to touch their lives in response to self-help.

Clay remembered how the first part of the parade route was touchingly interrupted as two small school girls in sparkling, white dresses halted their progress to present him and his boss with large bouquets of flowers, a gesture which could only be appropriately acknowledged with hugs and kisses, that generated even more cheers from the crowd. Under the street banners and to the strains of music from the local band, they finally climbed the stairs of the Community building, and the crowd filled the street in front of them. Hundreds of people seemed like thousands to Clay that day.

After the speeches and when the crowd had gone its way, nothing could stop his pent-up emotion. And the toasts of strong local liquor to Kennedy and Ecuador and America burned his throat. The liquor didn't cause the tears.

Clay had slept a good while. And the Tiptons stirred to life, too. It was 9:45 p.m., Tokyo time, less than thirty minutes out. This was the Land of the Rising Sun, he thought, and he still hadn't seen one. In fact, he missed one en route and the last sunrise he saw was in Washington yesterday morning.

Their plane touched down late at 11 P.M. Clay, Bruce and Anne shook hands all around and said their goodbyes. They chatted as they deplaned and Clay encouraged them to consider Hong Kong.

"If we can make it, we'll look you up at the Hilton," Bruce assured him.

Through-passengers, like Clay, gathered in a crowded room and awaited their bus downtown. It finally was ready for loading and they piled in. It rolled out of the airport that night and Clay was sure that the surrounding countryside looked much like any other airport. It wasn't until they got closer to the city that Clay began to appreciate it.

The ride through the industrial section took half an hour and they unloaded at a beautiful hotel, the New Ohtani, in downtown Tokyo before 1 A.M.

The hotel was so large that it boasted two thousand rooms, but his was tiny. Even the bed was small, just too short to really stretch out in it. He feared his toes would be permanently curled as he struggled with the end of the mattress and tightly-tucked sheets. His best thoughts were to make the most of the sights and sounds in the morning before his brief Tokyo stopover ended and he headed back to the airport for the plane to Hong Kong.

He slept fitfully. Nightmares. Awake every hour, he got up at 5 A.M. It just started to get light then, though it was very cloudy and stormy looking, but no rain. There were gigantic skyscrapers off in the distance, which looked very much like what he imagined to be Tokyo's Wall Street.

He sat down in a chair and looked out the windows from twenty stories up and reflected on the ride into the city last night. It all reminded him of what a giant, human honeycomb must be like inside: winding streets and underpasses, British-style traffic patterns, every square inch seemingly used for something. Yet, out the windows that morning, there were beautiful clusters of large trees very near this hotel in the heart of the city. What a happy surprise, Clay thought.

In the lobby early to wait for breakfast service to begin, there was a change of weather from clouds to sunlight. He passed up the Azalea Coffee Shop in favor of the Rose Room and he was welcomed inside.

His small table was on a slight rise from the main floor, in a perfect place to view the typical Japanese garden, bathed in sunlight, just outside the picture windows of the dining room.

Everything on his table was perfectly set, including the placement of a delicate flower in a vase. The bright sun caught his white tablecloth and bounced off his utensils. They were strangely oversized and, for that reason, didn't fit the scene. Rather, they reminded him of the decorator spoon-

and-fork pieces hung on the wall. But nothing could
have improved the garden that caught his eyes more
often than his breakfast plate. The manicured lawn
and plantings were of brilliant colors in the morning
light, now highlighting the entire garden, complete
with pagoda and red-railed foot bridge, gently
arched over a pond.

He was also attracted to an elderly Japanese
couple seated nearby. He had pure white hair and
was dressed in a Western business suit. She wore
traditional robes, fine silk and beautiful. He was a
tall and handsome Japanese; she, diminutive and
delicate.

Clay glanced at him again. He sat ramrod
straight. Years ago, in the great battles of the Pacific,
he may have been an officer on a battleship or, more
likely, an aircraft carrier in battle formation against
U.S. naval forces. Or, he was a Colonel, perhaps,
leading hordes of Japanese soldiers trained for am-
phibious assaults on American bases on tiny island
dots, crossing the endless ocean from Hawaii to the
Philippines. Or, maybe he was a life-long businessman. But, in any event, Clay certainly had no cause
to feel personal animosity now toward that man. Nor
should he. There was no war or fight in progress now.
He felt, in fact, a sense of respect. Time, itself, had
transformed their respective countries from old bitter enemies into new and stalwart allies. But, he
wouldn't forget that man, nor his submissive-ap-
pearing companion.

This tranquil, peaceful scene in the sunlit breakfast room was worth the long flight. He sat and

savored the surroundings and thoughts of his being in Tokyo. It seemed as though he was a million miles from home and further yet from Middlesex Beach and the beach house on another ocean around the world.

But, thoughts of the quest were very much with him at his table that bright morning. And it seemed so incongruous as he caught himself reviewing the rules of the hunt in his mind as he sat in the midst of the splendor of this room. He felt that the thrill of the hunt was cluttering his full appreciation of the scene before him. Or, was it the other way around? Maybe all this strange beauty imposed on his concentration for it. He became aware that some of his fellow passengers slowly departed their tables and headed for the cashier. The bus waited outside the huge lobby to take them back to the airport and their flight to Hong Kong. Not being able to tarry longer, he reluctantly folded his napkin and placed it on the table. He took one more long look out the windows to the garden. This was, indeed, the Land of the Rising Sun. How very beautiful. He picked up his check and headed for the lobby.

As the bus rolled through the city, his eyes saw the unseen sights of last night's trip to the hotel. They wove in and out among the skyscrapers, past hurrying crowds on foot and a tangle of motor traffic on urgent business in modern, downtown Tokyo. Slowly, the scene changed to freeways and more open areas as the city faded in the background and soon the control tower of the airport was framed in the windshield of the spotless, new bus.

In the few minutes before the soft hiss of the air brakes stopped their bus at the Pan Am entrance, he had time to wonder again at his folly. Why had he taken this gamble?

In the old days, he passed through Las Vegas a number of times and played the slots a little and threw a few dollars on the crap tables. When someone else rolled the dice for an eight, his favorite bet was a hard eight, two fours. The odds were ten-to-one, and he often won.

Once, he even took a bus to Atlantic City for the day and walked away with a hundred dollars of their money stuffed into his right boot. But, now, he had bet two thousand dollars on winning a million.

He damn near panicked as he waited in one of the endless lines at the Pan Am counter. After nearly an hour as he inched his heavy too-many-pieces of luggage along the floor in a sea of travelers, he discovered that he was in the wrong line. He picked up all his junk and figured he'd never make his flight. Finally, an airline representative guided him a little and he got rid of most of the bulky luggage at a check-in.

As he waited at the gate for his flight to be called, he struck up a conversation with a retired fisheries expert now based in California. He was headed for Hong Kong, too. After a while they climbed into another 747 for the four hour flight. The retiree was in first-class, however. That was what retirement and a retainer from a private firm did for you. It was something to look forward to, he thought, as he left his lucky companion and headed toward the tail of the plane.

And then they were up and away. As they passed through a little turbulence, he remembered last night, as he stood in yet another line to go through customs in Tokyo. The lady in front of him asked what he thought of the rough ride for an hour or so on the in-bound flight. He told her, bravely, that it wasn't too bad.

"I thought we were going to crash," she said.

"You should think positively," Clay told her.

"I did! I thought we were going to crash!!"

Hong Kong was much more than Clay expected. It was bigger and even more beautiful than he had imagined. He couldn't look at the clusters of modern, tall buildings surrounding the island's harbor without thinking of finance and business and wealth and power. And he was struck immediately with the knowledge that he stood on a piece of the once earth-girdling British Empire, which tenaciously held onto that leased land for so long, a stone's throw from the People's Republic of China. That tiny British colony, to be turned over July 1, 1997, was negotiated between representatives of China and Britain, and it seemed so ill-placed geographically in the face of China's vast land mass. It was a pebble on the shore; it was a David at Goliath's gigantic doorway.

At the Hilton, Clay picked up his conference folder from Bob, the coordinator, who met him at his door in his bathrobe. He had the flu – Hong Kong, maybe. The privacy of Clay's own spacious room on the 19th floor and the need to unpack his gear gave him ample time to peruse the thick schedule folder. Besides an agenda and background papers, he found a guest card for the China Fleet Club and an invitation to a reception to be given by the American Consul General. Clay's first appointment was to be breakfast tomorrow with Bob and a brief shopping tour with Bob's local Chinese friend, who knew, of course, the best places to buy. The boss would be coming into Hong Kong from Jakarta later in the week and would join them for a working dinner to focus on the conference. Bob's suggestion that Clay should see the show on the top floor was ignored in favor of his bed, which, even then, looked so inviting.

Having missed dinner, Clay awoke about 6 A.M. He was worn out by the trip and the kid-like excitement he felt at being in Hong Kong. Out his window, on a street far below, was an old Chinese man doing his exercises, slow and graceful stretches of arms and legs from a standing position. He was in the sun to get the full benefit of the warmth of the new day. Clay watched him for a time before starting his own exercise routine. He was not so lean as the man outside.

Later that morning, Clay and one of his colleagues signed up for a bus tour of the so-called New Territories. Awaiting bus time, they walked a block or so from the hotel to take the tram up Victoria Mountain to the overlook of the harbor, but the crowd lined up for the same spectacular view they

sought now circled the block. Besides, it was humid
as hell. The crowd and weather were like at the base
of the Washington Monument in D.C.

Clay thought that the seventy-six mile bus trip
was time and eight dollars Hong Kong well spent.
The new, air-conditioned bus took them to Kowloon
Peninsula and out Nathan Street to Boundary
Street where they entered the new Territories. Clay
got some pictures of the sampans, the small Chinese
boats which plied many waterways in the Orient,
and the people who sailed and lived on them. He saw
farmers in fields, beautiful fishing villages and most
of all, saw the people, zillions of them. At the furthest point of their tour, they climbed by foot a small,
very steep hill to get a view of Red China just on the
other side of a river in a beautiful valley. It was not
unlike other grand mountain scenes he had encountered in Oregon and Peru and Wyoming.

His friend outside the window next morning was
joined by another for their exercises. Right then it
looked as though they were swimming with their
toes dragging the bottom of an imaginary pool. Then
they circled their legs on what appeared to be joint-
less knees.

By noon, a number of Asian Bureau Office Directors had dropped by the headquarter's suite to renew
long friendships and to chat. It helped Clay to get
some of their interests and needs lined up for post
conference actions. Several of them later met in the

lobby for lunch and their group grew to about ten participants. This was the nucleus of the Asian Bureau. Clay probably learned more about its politics than he could in a month in Washington. He met a number of the new men he would meet again at country offices on the rest of the trip.

He had chosen the Spanish omelette lunch and it must have hit his stomach like a ton of bricks. After a quick nap, he made it to the boss's reception on the 4th floor at 6 P.M. in the Australia Room. He didn't dare touch any of the fancy foods but circulated and met most of the participants. By the time it ended, he had stuffed a lot of information into the back of his head and had received informal invitations to visit offices in India, Nepal and Pakistan next Spring. And the contacts and special problems in those countries had been noted.

He awoke at 3:30 the next morning. He wasn't sure whether it was still jet lag, the upset stomach or something that had been gnawing at him ever since "Win" had proposed the quest. Finally, as he sat on the edge of his bed, he remembered what it was that must have bothered him: "Win" had used the kids' example of a game and called it a treasure hunt. When Clay was in school, they called the game a scavenger hunt. So what, he said to himself as he walked over to the window and gazed out at the harbor lights. It was trivial. What difference did it make? The game was the same and just known by different names. Treasure hunt or scavenger hunt, this was much more. It paled the kids' name for it and Travis, Rog and he were committed to it. The big game was on. In fact, several days into it.

He switched on the TV and happened to catch an early weather report: there was a typhoon building up, rather fast, in the area but it didn't sound very threatening to him. Too far away. He turned it off and went back to bed.

After breakfast, Bob and Clay were in the conference room, the first of the forty-four participants to attend the opening session. As they waited, Bob said that the typhoon was expected to hit Hong Kong at noon today.

"Great Caesar!" Clay said, "It didn't sound that serious early this morning!"

"Before I left my room, I heard on the news that the ferries have stopped running, schools are closed and most businesses won't open," Bob offered.

The scene outside the twenty-fifth floor windows of the conference room was in stark contrast to the past few days of bright and warm weather. It just began to rain and was gray then.

The morning's first speaker gave some late information on Typhoon Elsie, along with other bad news preceding his briefing on China. He announced, regretfully, the cancelling of the reception and planned musical presentation by Chinese dancers at his residence because of the storm. Elsie, he said, was scheduled to hit Hong Kong at 1 P.M. today. She would be Clay's first typhoon.

As the briefing continued, Clay glanced outside and could see that many of the windows on the top floor of the hotel had been taped to prevent flying glass. The conference room had not. Clay could hardly see the harbor now and the wind was really howling.

The morning session was finally at an end. Clay sat there a little nervous about the strong winds and rain that hit the windows some six feet from him. And he wondered how those people out there in the countless sampans, violently bobbing at the edge of Kowloon and Hong Kong harbor, were making out. Badly, he suspected.

Lunch break only confirmed that there was no traffic moving outside. No one was leaving or entering the hotel. Back in the conference room, the rain was now blowing so hard against the windows that one could hardly see out. The howl and the whistle of the wind on the windows were so loud that they could barely hear what was being said in the room. It seemed much worse to Clay than the hurricane he was in one November at the beach in Delaware. But, it was still predicted that it would be over that night. It seemed very strange to him not to see people and the traffic out there and the boats that moved back and forth across the harbor. When the rain abated a minute, he looked down and saw a tree lying across the road in front of the hotel. Other debris bobbed in pools of water.

A hell of a time for a first trip to Hong Kong, he thought.

After the coffee break, the boss reassured them by saying that the hotel management had told him that the wind was hitting the building full force from the opposite side and they weren't foolheartedly sitting there getting the brunt of the storm. They also learned that the storm was now passing thirty miles from Hong Kong. Clay wondered how much play, if any, Typhoon Elsie got in The Washington Post.

Clay jumped again into the renewed discussions by asking a question about guidelines regarding the participation of the private sector in development programs and it touched off a rather lively exchange. At the end of the time devoted to the subject, the boss said that it should be included in the report on the highlights of the conference. Clay's points didn't go unheeded.

They were told that they would be confined to the hotel because of the storm. Clay headed for the bar after the meeting ended and joined other participants to continue conference topics. When the discussion became more and more pointless because of gin and scotch that slurred the speakers' tongues and distorted their declarations, Clay slipped away and had room service bring a big pot of hot Chinese noodle soup to the nineteenth floor and flipped on his TV for storm news.

He was surprised by the pictures of wide-spread damage to trees, buildings and small shops on the streets of Hong Kong and Kowloon. The wind damage was extensive. Elsie had come closest to the island at 2 P.M., just as their afternoon session was getting underway. Winds got as high as 110 miles per hour and they issued the #10, the highest storm warning, called the hurricane signal, for the first time in four years.

As he took another invitation from the conference folder, Clay slowly re-read it and tossed it into the wastepaper basket. That one was for the planned trip for delegates by hydrofoil boats to Macao for a night at the casino, also cancelled. He would only dream of seeing that South China Sea island.

What in hell, he asked himself, should he be looking for in Hong Kong to offer up on his list to give to "Win" by the 30th? He had no idea.

He fell into bed with the storm on his mind, filled with scenes of trees bending and flaying in the violent wind and driving rain, of demolished buildings, of debris-filled streets and flooding.

Right on schedule, he was awake at four again and stood and looked from his window at the rain. He was sure that his Chinese friends wouldn't be able to exercise again that morning and, like him, were prisoners in some safe haven waiting for Elsie to get out of range and for Hong Kong to return to normal.

The first one in the coffee shop, he shuffled some papers from his folder to check the morning speakers. Nine directors would give their country reports, making for a long day. But the overviews should be helpful and interesting. In one day, he would get updated information on the economic picture in nine Asian countries, many of them in the path of his travel route at the conclusion of this conference. And he surmised that everything would be downhill in the course of his visits to those developing areas of the Orient after the glamour and sophistication and evidence of immense wealth enjoyed by many in

Hong Kong. Though the social engagements there were curtailed by the storm, he thought of what the reception at the residence and the casino night at Macao would have been like and hoped that things would pick up after Hong Kong to enliven the trip.

Though he would learn the facts and figures, the nuts-and-bolts of the economies of the area, he was anxious to see how they worked in practice and to meet the movers and shakers, both locals and Americans, in the field and break out of the tedium of these working sessions. He wanted to see the people and feel the pulse of the cultures wherever he went in the Far East and in Europe, just as he had experienced it much earlier in Latin America.

Clay was joined at breakfast by their representative in Korea who told him that he had arranged to put him up at an army compound in Seoul and would have a schedule of meetings ready when he arrived. Also, a car to meet him to take him to quarters. Seoul was to be his first stop after the conference, which would wind up in a couple of days.

It was raining again as they entered the conference room. The country reports began with Indonesia followed by Korea, the Philippines and Thailand. All would be on Clay's itinerary after Hong Kong. So he listened to each presentation and tried to stay alert and take notes. In Indonesia, for example, its private sector was weak in contrast with the Philippines; it was a leader in the Third World and the only East Asian country capable of moving into a power role; it had experienced poor management of investments; and, even though it was a member of OPEC, the oil producing bloc, one-half of its population earned less than one hundred dollars a year, the poorest in the area.

After four countries and then a roast beef sandwich lunch, with a Hong Kong beer, they were back at it again. The rain was picking up. In fact, it poured out there. The bleakness and the disheartening, persistent rain outside matched the sketch he listened to on Bangladesh: with eighty million people now, its population would double by 2005; they earned seventy dollars per capita; seventy percent of U.S. assistance was for food; and the resultant discouragement of migrators to urban areas and camps would send masses of people back again to the barren land. The gloomy reports on Pakistan, Nepal, India and Sri Lanka only further dampened Clay's spirits.

Tucked neatly into the back of his mind, at every meeting, during each speaker's boring presentation, at each cocktail party, lunch and dinner, was the quest. The quest. It was the thing that kept him alert, thinking, planning, looking, wondering. It was a secret, pleasing, hidden diversion, kept tightly within its bounds lest it try to take full rein of his every wakeful thought. It was his, alone, to control. It was frightening. And he knew he would carry it, everywhere, for nearly a month. But, on top of it all, he knew that he had to have decent country backgrounds in his head to make the rest of the business part of the trip as productive as possible. After all, that was what he was being paid to do and do well. And there were other tasks he told no one.

The afternoon meeting broke up at 6:30 and he hurried to his room to change for dinner. The young hotel sales manager was taking five of them to the Lychee Village, a superb Chinese restaurant, he said, a short distance from the hotel.

Clay mused that the infighting at the conference had helped to spice it. You could see and feel it at every gathering. There were lots of prima donnas and as many personality clashes and, though the conference tone had been noted for a discussion of the issues and the leadership had encouraged personal participation by everyone, some of the sessions had exploded with heated exchanges.

As he waited in the lobby for the rest of the party, Clay strolled by the desk and left his key. The desk clerk was about to put the key in the slot and pulled out a letter and handed it to Clay. It was from Jamie. He sat down and read it. It was a sweet brief note. He didn't need her note to remind him of her. She had been on his mind, too.

Just then, Phil walked up and sat down with Clay to chat and wait for the others. Phil, the sales manager, was twenty-seven and said he expected to retire at a young thirty-six. He reminded Clay of a dark-complexioned, suave Sigma Chi brother of his from college days. Both had that certain class and confidence and smarts in proportions adequate to reach their goals in life. Clay wasn't aware of the fortunes of his fraternity brother but, in their short acquaintance, he had great respect for the forward-looking Phil, whose mother was Chinese and father American. The hotel would have been hard pressed to find a more handsome, gregarious man than Phil in a sales role at the Hilton.

The six of them piled into the hotel's Rolls Royce parked at the entrance and took the short ride in the evening traffic to the restaurant. Phil was right about the food. They had lobster, beef, squid, chicken, duck, pork, vegetables and an almond custard pudding. They had enjoyed good dinner conversation on topics other than the conference and afterward, several of them, including Clay, walked back to the hotel. Clay bought two candy bars in the lobby before going to his room. He figured he might get hungry in the night.

After the final day's sessions, Clay and Tom, one of the conference delegates from Washington, tried Jimmy's Kitchen for dinner. Located near the hotel, Clay hoped to satisfy his craving for some plain Chinese noodle soup but he got a watered-down Campbell's variety, which wasn't what he had in mind.

"Why in hell can't I get a decent bowl of Chinese noodles in Hong Kong like I get in Washington, D.C.?" Clay asked.

"Damned if I know," Tom said as he dipped into the sweet and sour pork on a large plate in the middle of their table.

"All I wanted was a bowl of noodles, topped with strips of pork roast, egg slices and chopped green onions and I get a poor substitute here in Hong Kong that wouldn't even be on the menu in D.C."

"Maybe that style noodle dish originated in D.C. rather than in China!"

Finishing the tasty pork, they had their fill of tea and walked the streets of Hong Kong till midnight. They visited the bars in a little district on the island but were more impressed with the street scenes than the B-girls. High up on the sides of what they'd call tenement houses or high-rise buildings in large U.S. cities, they saw rows of washed clothes hanging parallel to every floor, practically encircling entire buildings. Had Clay's little Mother seen it, she would have jokingly said that the Chinese were either very dirty or very clean. It was like colorful bunting, hung for a parade or a national holiday, fluttering in the breezes. Or, if there were balconies, multi-colored patches of clothing were draped, floor upon floor, over the railings until it appeared that the buildings were wrapped in gaily patterned paper to camouflage what was inside.

At street level, canopied stands and sidewalk markets often impeded foot traffic on narrower streets and giant, brightly colored umbrellas which shielded some, required that you watched your head as you craned your neck to inspect the vast assortment of food and wares. Tiny grocery store fronts dotted block after block of vending areas, which were everywhere.

And the streetwagons, complete with stoves that emitted white smoke, hauled huge, steaming pots and laden with all kinds of clanging cooking utensils, attracted customers with the odors of boiling rice and cooking fish and chicken. It all seemed better to Clay than Jimmy's Kitchen.

The lean kids and running dogs and old men and rickshaws, some idle and some with owners trotting by, all blended into a frantic scene of sights, sounds and smells. What a place this was! Clay was glad that Tom and several others would remain there in Hong Kong a few more days with him so that they could explore and wander and shop before Korea. This was the respite needed after long conference hours to unwind and appreciate this famous island. At their walk's end, though, Clay was ready for some sleep and went up to his room.

He switched on his TV and took off his jacket when the phone rang.

"Yes?"

"Clay? This is Bruce."

"Bruce! Where in hell are you?"

"Downstairs. We may need the assistance of your good offices to get a roof over our heads tonight."

"Full up?"

"That's what the desk clerk says."

"I'll slip down and see what I can do. Stay put!"

"Will do. Thanks."

Clay pulled on his jacket, grabbed his room key and closed the door behind him. He half-trotted down the hall to the elevator. Inside, he pushed the lobby button and, in the empty elevator practiced some exercise moves, Chinese-style. He was concentrating so hard on an arm and a leg extension that he almost kicked a matronly lady getting on at the tenth floor. He sheepishly grinned and straightened himself up as she glared in surprise, then smiled at him.

When the doors opened, the lady turned to him and said, "When you extend your leg, point with your toes!" and quickly walked into the lobby, as Clay smiled his thanks and headed for the registration desk.

The Tiptons warmly greeted Clay like a long-lost friend. Anne gave him a hug and a kiss on the cheek. He walked them over to Phil's office and hoped he could make good on his offer to help his new companions. Phil came through.

"If you cut red tape at the State Department like you do at the Hong Kong Hilton, you must be an indispensable man!" Bruce said as the three of them sat in comfortable chairs at a table in the lobby lounge.

"Phil just knew something they didn't know at the desk," Clay said and lifted his glass. "To the Tiptons and welcome to the Hilton!" he toasted.

"Here's to you, Clay," Anne smiled. "You found room for us at the inn! Thanks."

"How long can you folks stay?"

"Only till Friday. Bruce ended the stint in Tokyo a couple of days early and we made some reservations on Pan Am, taking what we could get in and out of Hong Kong. But I'm thrilled with the chance to see this place."

"Well, that gives you a few days anyway. The conference is over for me and I can spend some time with you, if you like, doing some sightseeing. I really haven't had a chance yet, except for a walk or two."

"What we don't see on our own," Bruce said, "we'll see together. That will be great."

"Save the China Fleet Club for me," Clay said. "I'll arrange to get two more guest cards. I understand they have quite a selection of items there."

"Sounds good," Bruce said, and the three chatted another hour.

Clay joined the Tiptons to shop and to ascend Victoria Mountain for the view and, when Mr. Chen, the Chinese businessman he had met on his second day in Hong Kong was introduced to Bruce and Anne, the genial Chinese invited them to join the party for dinner on their last night in town. They accepted.

Mr. Chen picked them up, along with Clay, in his car at the Hilton and took them to the Yung Kee restaurant. The Yung Kee, one of the top ten in Hong Kong, consisted of five floors of food service. It was an attractive place and Clay noticed at once the family-oriented nature of the immense eatery. It seemed that many tables consisted of at least one white-haired grandfather and grandmother down to the smallest grandchildren in a party of ten or twelve or more. And the most memorable things about the groups were the smiles, laughter and pure enjoyment of these families as they dined out.

Their meal started with beer and tea. When not listening to Mr. Chen as he outlined a schedule of shopping and sightseeing still in store for him, and when not conversing with the Tiptons and the rest of the party, Clay's eyes swept over the crowded room. Waiters and waitresses, who pushed wheeled carts stacked with varied sizes of wooden bowls filled with steaming food, passed to and fro among the throng of diners, dispensed tasty dishes and stacked empties from the tables nearby. Their own table was soon crowded with dishes of duck, pork, fried rice, sweet and sour, chicken chow mein and a noodle soup close to Clay's favorite. And when the meal was finished, they were served a shallow, tiny cup of very strong tea. The surprising climax to the dining room service procedure was when the waiter figured the bill by counting the empty bowls near their table. Very clever these Chinese, Clay thought, as he enjoyed his admiration when their party left the restaurant.

At the hotel, he and the Tiptons said goodbye since their flight left very early in the morning.

"I'll see you back in Washington," Clay said.

"We hope so."

Clay was surprised to get a call the next morning from Mr. Chen in the lobby. "Mr. Stevenson, there was a package left in my car last night and there is a card on it addressed to you."

"Really? I'll be down to pick it up, Mr. Chen."

"Thanks so much."

Back in his room, Clay read the card in the envelope:

"Clay – You made our stay in HK a truly rewarding experience and we will treasure it. This gift is with our thanks. Anne"

Clay opened the small package in brown wrapping paper. Inside the flimsy, cardboard box was a brass statue of Mi-lo Fo, the Laughing Buddha. That

Anne! he thought. She knew that he would love to
have a memento of Hong Kong. A brass collector, he
turned it upside down to see if it bore any markings
of where it was made. As he did, something rattled
inside. Hell! he said aloud. Could the salesman have
sold Anne a defective statue with a chunk of loose
brass clunking around in there, he wondered? Anyway, there was no mark on the bottom so it couldn't
be a very old piece, he thought. He knew that he
would never tell Anne that the damn thing clunked.
He looked at the workmanship and, for good luck,
stroked the brass figure's fat, shiny belly with his
fingers, wrapped it in a small towel and put it into
his briefcase.

Clay joined up with Tom after breakfast and
they set out on foot looking for the perfect pearl
rings. They made their way through the crowded
streets and, after a few wrong turns and backtracks,
found the jewelry store. They had been given good
advice because they both bought quality pearls to
suit their shopping lists and their self-imposed price
limitations.

Their newest Chinese friend in Hong Kong was
one of the island's most outstanding and popular
jockeys. A handsome young guy, he and Mr. Chen
suggested going by car to visit a certain outlying
market area and then take the drive to Repulse Bay.

Since this was their last day in Hong Kong, they agreed.

The market made Clay think of the ones he had seen in many parts of Latin America. Only the sound of the language told him he wasn't in Lima or Guatemala City. They parked and walked through the colorful bazaar-like stands displaying countless varieties of fruits and vegetables, together with other sections devoted to handcrafted and manufactured items of every description. It must have been one of the island's more popular market places for the crowds were huge. Their guides had suggested that they might enjoy the flavor of the place and the visitors agreed that the "flavor" was considerable. Despite being in the open air, they were glad to escape the stifling heat of the crowded scene.

The visit to the Repulse Bay Hotel, a vintage landmark overlooking the sea, was a refreshing stop. They sat on the veranda and enjoyed dishes of ice cream to go with the magnificent view of the beach and feel the cooling breeze. Clay couldn't resist the opportunity to get a sample of sand for his collection. While the jockey phoned in their bets on his "sure thing" horse in one of the day's races, Clay went for a short walk on the shoreline.

Clay collected sand. It all started on his first trip to Costa Rica. While in the east coast port of Limon, he was fascinated by the extremely fine-grained black sand, which looked just like gunpowder. Then, traveling to the beach area at Puntarenas on Costa Rica's west coast, he found that the sand was brown.

Using 35 mm film cans to bring his samples home, he decided to start a sand collection.

He was sure that he wasn't the original sand-man, but he dared to say that he may be the only sand collector on the Virginia and Maryland coasts, and maybe throw in Delaware. The collection then consisted of samples from Europe, Asia, Africa and Latin America, representing some thirty countries, together with sand from all sections of the U.S.

And it just kept sifting in. People had brought him sand from places they had visited and people sent it to him. Recently he received a vial of sand from the base of the Sphinx and some from Uganda. One of his daughters remembered to bring him some sand from Myrtle Beach, South Carolina, on a vacation. In his travels, he had scooped up sample grains from the Mississippi, from San Francisco, the Oregon coast and from beaches up and down the East coast. Clay had sort of a standard ritual to prepare his samples for display. If it arrived wet or damp from the container, he spread it out on a plate in the sun to dry. It was then poured into a glass cigar tube, capped, labeled and placed in a display rack.

The real intrigue of it to him was that sand was not just sand. Of his samples, now numbering over one hundred fifty, none was like any other. He had closely examined many of them with a powerful magnifying glass and a good microscope.

Some of his observations: the sand from Bermuda was pink and very fine; sand from Pensacola was like salt; from Portugal, like coarse-ground pepper; from Niger in the African Sahara, it was light

brown and of face-powder texture; sand from the
Great Salt Lake rolled on a piece of paper because
each grain was like a bird egg; and the finest and
whitest was from St. Petersburg.

While over the years he has collected stamps,
coins and brass, he still felt caught up in the nitty-
gritty of sand. All of those granular specimens came
to mind as he walked on the beach at Repulse Bay.
And Clay wasn't kidding when he told Travis and
Rog once at the beach that his highest ambition was
to have some sand from the moon.

Looking up at the old hotel, he was impressed
by the grandeur of it, and sorry that the historic
building, dating back to the earliest British rule on
the island, was being squeezed and dwarfed by high-
rises all about it. But as long as the old hotel stood,
nothing could equal the splendid view it afforded
and the stirrings of history it inspired.

At dinner, the jockey paid Clay his winnings —
sixty cents on his two dollar bet. They ate dove,
shrimp rolls, pork, noodles and strong tea, but not
on Clay's winnings. Afterward, they walked the
streets to find a certain jewelry store and, when they
did, it was closed. They suddenly realized that they
were in the pickpocket district and hurried out of
there to the Hilton, where they said their goodbyes
to the two Chinese and thanked them for their time,
generosity and helpfulness in making it possible for
them to see more of the island.

How many jockeys do you meet in a lifetime?
That jockey, there in Hong Kong, with fame beyond
any Clay may possibly meet, was a unique fellow. He

was well-educated, as you could tell so easily in conversation, and immaculate in dress. His confidence showed through among strangers and Clay would never know why the jockey asked him what he had done in his working career before government. When Clay admitted to being a high school teacher for five years, the young man wanted to know all the details of that field. Clay tried to tell him how the teaching profession varied in parts of the U.S. and how it was viewed by administrators as well as teachers, and reflected the regionalism of the country. He told him the truth as he knew it.

Clay had reserved a car for 6:15 that morning to get to the airport. Tom would be going non-stop to San Francisco and thence home to Washington and Clay would be on his way to Korea.

Packing up, he had a scant fifteen minutes to get eggs and toast after checking out. His bill for eight days was over fifteen hundred dollars Hong Kong. The startling thing was not the size of the bill in local dollars, but that he suddenly realized he was ten days into the quest. One third of their time limit was gone. Only twenty days to get the rest of the way around the world and back to Middlesex. Great Caesar! Judging from the way time had flown thus far, he wondered, over his last sip of coffee, how he'd ever make it back in time.

The boss nabbed him by the arm on his way out and apologized for not meeting them that other night but that the Ambassador had ambushed him. Then Clay stuck his head into Phil's office and wished him good fortune.

He was a little sad on seeing Hong Kong for the last time on that trip as his car sped away from the hotel. Being Sunday, the streets were quite deserted at that time of morning, with only a few pedestrians and many newspaper vendors kneeling on the sidewalks, inserting supplements, just like in Washington, D.C. A brilliant sunrise greeted their day.

FOUR

Scholastically, Travis Goodson carried five major subjects his senior year and, while he hadn't earned straight A's, he graduated from high school with a grade average to match many classmates in the top 10% and was accepted at Stanford University. There, he suddenly dropped his participation in sports and chose the path to law, where he effectively employed his gift of gab and intellectual prowess as he made the vocational decision one usually makes at that juncture of life. At least, Travis made his choice right then and there and graduated with a law degree.

At the University, he met Ainsley, a journalism major and editor of the campus newspaper. They were married when they both graduated that same year. From that moment, Travis became a one-woman man, not one at a time. For, it was Ainsley he wanted and loved and their marriage, over the years, became one of those exceptional ones in which the man and the woman found fulfillment and joy and happiness in being together and loving together. In their unique compatibility and mutual devotion, there was no room for boredom.

Back home in Omaha, it wasn't long before the promising young lawyer developed an interest in politics and skipped the local level options which were opened very early to him. He was elected to the state Senate, the youngest in the history of the state. Not many years later, he found that practicing party politics impinged on his growth and full practice of the law, his greater love, and the family moved to Washington, D.C., where Travis could be closer to his specialty. At first, he missed his role in the state capital, but knew that he could broaden his horizons in the nation's capital.

"Brandy," Rog asked on the phone, "how did the meeting go at school?"

"Well, the meeting was in the principal's office because the counselor was sick this morning. Anyway, the registrar and the principal had worked out a schedule of five solids for Jimmy to graduate. He can do it if he eases up on all those sports. He's got to or he'll be in a pickle."

"He can do it. I'll have a talk with him."

"Really talk with him, Rog, and talk less about the Redskins and the Orioles till he gets on track this year."

In a North Carolina high school, Roger had one girl, Brandy, and he married her after he graduated from junior college. Then, with his bride, he went to the Medical School of Georgia in Augusta.

During his high school days, Rog was the student who made the best drawings of how to dissect a frog, loved all science and was a "brain" in the courses, was the "jitterbug" who sweat the most on the gym floor at the school dances and was valedictorian of his class. In junior college, he was the only Freshman who could drive his old flashy Model A Ford from the campus to town without using his hands – he shifted with his knees and steered with his elbows. He was a practical joker then and remained one. And he loved his beer and, a little less, poker games, and still did. He had excelled in Latin in high school and, when he got to college, wrote the most beautiful pages of German script the instructor ever saw. Some of those traits made Rog one of the brightest lights to graduate from medical school and, perhaps, all of them contributed to it.

"Helen, please see if you can get Brandy on the line," the doctor said, as he leafed through a patient's chart on the board he carried, as he passed her desk.

"Of course, Doctor."

Rog put the board in the middle of his desk and studied it. Poor Mrs. Smithers would have to have that operation on her broken hip this week, and the sooner the better. When the phone rang, he let the pages fall from his grasp and picked up the receiver.

"Brandy?"

"Hi, Rog. You caught me coming in the door with my arms full of groceries. Just a sec. I want to sit down and catch my breath. This shopping just wears me out any more. We must be getting older."

"So is everyone I know, Brandy. Even the little citizens an hour or two old I saw at the hospital this morning. Some of them with no names, but getting older every minute."

"Okay, Rog!"

"Brandy, how'd you like to join your handsome husband on a trip to London, Paris,..."

"Rog, did you have two martinis at lunch?"

"Listen, it's all falling together faster than I can tell you! My esteemed associate has agreed to delay his vacation so that you and I can get away together now."

"You mean he came down off his high horse long enough to give you a break? I can't believe it!"

"Well, he also knows about the proposition with 'Win' and I've got to get going on that."

"What do you know! I can't believe it!"

"Also, I just heard that a doctor from Johns Hopkins has agreed to start work at the clinic tomorrow. A Dr. White. He was going to Atlanta after Hopkins, but has decided to work for a while in our clinic before making the move South."

"Rog this is all so sudden..."

"Brandy, try and calm down. We'll decide how to handle the kids while we're gone and get our airline tickets. I'll be home early this afternoon so we can get on with it."

"This isn't a prank of yours, is it? I couldn't stand it!"

"Brandy, we're going to Europe! In just a few days!"

"Come home, Rog."

"I'll be there soon."

Driving home, Rog thought of some of his early pranks. Brandy had thought this trip was one! But, it was for real.

Once, when his next door neighbor was house painting, Rog put a for sale ad in the paper for it. Every time the neighbor was out on the ladder the damn phone would ring and he'd have to come down to answer. Or, the time he had a dead tree planted in a friend's yard – in concrete. Another neighborly stunt was to have a load of cow manure delivered while a couple was out of town. But, somehow, his friendships endured. He was often glad that his beach house was still unmolested and at a safe distance from reprisals. He was more proud of it than his Baltimore home.

At the beach house, he had built a replica of an English pub with his own hands and loved to entertain and cut-up at the bar, as well as to tinker at woodwork when he was away from the clinic, especially at the beach.

And, too, he was some kind of cook! Why, he made an English dish or two better than the English, and he knew it. He wasn't the gourmet that some were, but he liked to keep his hand in the kitchen arts.

Though Brandy didn't like him cluttering the counters all that much, she tolerated it. Rog loved to cook breakfast on weekends when they were at Middlesex, for his two teenage daughters. And it encouraged them to give Dad some help in the kitchen, too, a break from helping their Mom in that department.

Because of the doctor in him, he hoped this European trip would give a lift to Brandy. He had been worried about her irritability lately and often blamed his own foolishness and outlandish antics, as well as his long hours, for wearing on her too much. With that on his mind, he would just have to bear his own pressures at the clinic a little better and not explode at her. Now, with a new thirty-day, self-inflicted deadline in the quest to cope with, he knew, as he pulled up to his house, that he'd have to suffer the heat mostly by himself and show Brandy, at the same time, some good fun on the trip. She needed it more than he did.

"Have you got any hugs, Brandy?" he said as he came into the kitchen, and she practically fell into his arms. He held her long and tenderly and he could almost feel her suppressed sobs. He kissed her cheek very lightly and then her lips. She responded with arms tightening around him and he knew, in that instant, that she was showing more love and affection than she had dared in a long time. For sure, he thought, I must make this a lovely trip for her.

Rosalie, a daughter, came in from watching TV in the family room and said, "Hi, Dad!"

"Hi, honey," Rog said, still holding Brandy very tight.

"Mom, okay for me to set the table now? Is dinner about ready?"

"Just about. Yes, go ahead and call Sue and ask her to unload the dishwasher. Dad and I are going to talk in the living room a minute," she said, stepped back and took Rog's hand, and led him into the other room. As they sat down on the sofa, she brushed her lips on his cheek.

"How long will we be in Europe?" she asked.

"Let's shoot for three weeks, at least. Maybe more. Okay?"

"Wonderful. You know I need to get away with you."

"And I want to be with you."

"Do you think Mother will stay with the kids?"

"I'm sure she will. Give her a call. Can you be ready to go in a couple of days? Is that pushing you too fast?"

"I'm ready now."

Travis left his office a little ahead of the evening traffic and the drive up Connecticut Avenue to Military Road was faster than usual. He took a right and headed for his house on Northampton Street, N.W., as radio announcers chattered on the car radio all the way. He pulled up into his driveway after the twenty minute ride and took the stairs two at a time to the front door. Ainsley was in the hallway by the door as he opened it and he grabbed her up in his arms and swung her around till she shrieked in delight.

"Travis! Travis! I'm losing a shoe!" she yelled, happily.

"Good! I'll buy you another pair in Panama and a new hat to go with them!"

Jamie and "Win" were seated in chaise lounges on the deck, outside the game room, as a wispy cloud moved across the full moon on a warm, early September evening. The stereo softly played and they lightly held hands. Juan came onto the deck and asked if they'd like a cocktail before dinner.

"I'd like scotch on the rocks, Juan, with some water."

"Make mine a bourbon and water," "Win" said. "When did you start drinking scotch, Jamie?"

"I tried one in Washington the other day at the Mayflower," she told him.

"How was your shopping trip, dear?"

"The weather was so dreadful I didn't get much done."

"The weather is always dreadful in Washington in August."

"But, I love Washington, and seeing the monuments at night, all with lights that make them look so very special and beautiful. And the shops. The whole city seems so open. You never see the tall, ugly, dirty buildings like in Philadelphia and New York. It's such a nice change."

As Juan served the drinks, he told "Win" that there was a call for him.

"I'll take it in the family room, Juan. Please excuse me a moment, Jamie, my dear."

"Win" walked quickly through the game room and the adjoining doorway, lifted the receiver and sat down in a Queen Anne chair.

"This is 'Win' Agar."

"Good evening, 'Win'."

"Good evening, Senator."

"Did they all get away?"

"Yes. One is in Central America, another in Europe and you know about the one in the Far East."

"Excellent, 'Win.' Goodnight."

"Goodnight."

"Brandy," Rog said, seated behind the wheel of the right-hand drive Ford, speeding down the motorway on their way to Bath, "I just had a beautiful thought."

"What about?"

"Clay."

"What made you think of him all of a sudden?"

"Well, he's out there on this mission alone. I have you!"

"Maybe he figured that's an advantage, not having a wife along to worry about on his trip. Did you think of that?"

"I thought of that. That's why I think we have the advantage. So does Travis, with Ainsley."

"It just seems like Clay'd have even more time to concentrate on the whole thing alone."

"Brandy, two heads are better than one! He may be out there digging around, wondering all about it to himself! But, the two of us can look and think, and, you know, talk it out, and analyze whatever we may come across. Clay can only agonize alone, unless he lets his hair down with a colleague about what he's looking for and trying to do, but I think he's too proud for that. He'd probably rather be a loner, but he'll suffer."

"You sure you wouldn't want to be here alone, too?"

"If I'm going to find four things of value on this trip, I'll need you. And I'm happy we're together on this."

"I'm so glad."

"Another thing, Clay is working. We're not! To me, that adds up to a double-barreled advantage."

"You may be right."

"You bet I'm right!"

In the few days since they had landed at Heathrow Airport near London, Rog and Brandy had been having a wonderful time. It had turned out to be a second honeymoon. Rog had promised her one long ago and now, after several canceled trips, they were together away from house, kids and clinic.

They stayed at an intimate, small hotel in Kensington and took the Underground to Piccadilly Circus and Trafalgar Square; visited a pub or two; lunched at small restaurants, where Rog could sample his favorite dishes and try the flat White fish; saw the Changing of the Guard at Buckingham Palace; stood in the House of Commons at the Parliament Buildings on the Thames, and walked around the corner to Westminster Abbey; were startled by the ravens on a nearby wall as they toured the Tower of London; and shopped at Harrods. They were tourists and loved it.

One night, in their room, Rog read an original poem he had started on the trip. Brandy thought it was pretty good. It began:

We went to merry England,
To see old London town,
The shops, the spires were everywhere,
We saw the British crown.
The Parliament, inspiring!
A symbol of free men,
We saw the bench and stood in awe,

Where Churchill rallied them.

And then they made, or at least they thought so, their first mistake – they rented a car. Rog had one hell of a time getting the hang of the thing. Everything was backward on it, at least on the wrong side.

And driving on the left was terror at first, too. They had both run the car up on the left-hand curbs a couple of times. Asking directions and trying to follow them were two different things: where circles became roundabouts; interstates were motorways; and two-way highways, dual carriageways. They bought a bunch of maps and booklets and made up their minds that there was a lot more to see than just London. Checking out of their hotel, they hit the road and headed for Hampton Court, the palace of Henry VIII. Along the way, they laughed about it and speculated that good, experienced American drivers like themselves, soon became bad beginners and a menace.

Hampton Court was magnificent and they toured it inside and out. Rog was fascinated by the tennis courts because he used to teach the game in college. Those earlier experiences hit him when he viewed the courts used by Henry. It was hard to imagine that the most famous of English Kings played tennis on those very courts! It was easier to envision George Washington at Mount Vernon than Henry VIII, there. Perhaps it was because he preceded Washington by over 250 years on history's stage, for everything that Rog saw at Hampton Court was taking his eyes back nearly 500 years. After spending some extra time in the extensive gardens, which Brandy loved, and taking photographs, they checked their maps and headed for Bath.

Though they had asked other visitors at Hampton Court for advice on the best way to get to Bath, they found that all of them had been wrong on the time it took to make the drive. They were told everywhere from "several hours" to "you can't possibly drive there before dark." It was actually an easy, rather short trip and they arrived in late afternoon, well before dark.

Brandy was driving when they entered the city and she was nervous as they got into the unusual traffic patterns, including the one-way streets of Bath. Rog was frantically trying to watch the road and street map at the same time in his attempt to steer them to a hotel near the ancient Roman baths. Brandy nearly became hysterical and yelled, "Which way?" and "What do I do?" as Rog shouted new directions. After two or three passes around several blocks to get on a street near the hotel, he finally told her, in desperation, to stop the car. She stopped by a curb at a busy intersection and Rog got out and ran to the nearest startled pedestrian to ask if he could direct them out of their predicament. Back at the car, Rog told Brandy to let him take the wheel and give a try at getting them to the hotel by following the new directions.

"What did he say?"

"Brandy, I'll forget if I try to repeat it. Just let me drive!"

They finally got on the right street by the hotel and parked. They were drained. They just sat a few minutes before getting out of the car to carry their luggage into the hotel and register. Fortunately, a room was available.

Upstairs, Brandy propped pillows behind Rog's back as he leaned against the headboard on the bed. Then she hurried down the hall to the ice machine and, back in the room, got the bottle of Three Crown gin from the carrying bag and poured two gins over ice.

"Maybe we should have taken a bus instead of renting that damn car," Rog said, wearily.

"The car gives us more flexibility. We'll get used to driving in a few days." She hoped, especially, that she would.

"But, every road we would get on would be strange to us. It's wearing us out!"

"Relax and drink your drink. Traffic will be easier to handle as we go along. Now, you relax."

Brandy sat on the other side of the bed, put a pillow behind her back and kicked off her shoes. They both sat and drank their gin and had a laugh or two over the trip.

"Are you mad because I told you to stop the car down there on the street?"

"No! I was so confused and frustrated I couldn't think! I just hope the local citizens aren't too upset!"

"Well, we made it. We made it to our safe little room. Is there more ice?"

Brandy took his glass and scooped up more ice into it from the plastic bucket and poured the gin. Then she filled her own.

"We don't have a jigger, vermouth, a twist or olives," she said, "but who cares? Let's drink this and nap a while and then go have a fabulous dinner."

"Sounds wonderful."

"Want to get under the covers?"

"Love to."

Bath was charming English beauty at its best. The city embraced the old and the very old with style. To Rog and Brandy, the spectacular Royal Crescent, which they saw on an evening walking tour, offered a perfect example of Georgian town planning. And the fifteenth century Abbey, while small, with its exterior lighting showing the intricate detail, made a deep impression on them.

But the visit to the Roman ruins surrounding the mineral waters, which had gushed from below the earth's crust through 2000 years of continuous use, unvarying in temperature and quantity, was the highlight of their two days in Bath. Tea in the eighteenth century Pump Room was unforgettable. As Roman soldiers before them, they threw coins in the waters for good fortune before leaving for the North West.

Rog considered the English countryside to be the most picturesque he had ever seen. The irregular stone fences, the shades of green in grasses and croplands and the serenity of it all made each scene an enlargement from a calendar. Despite the tenseness when they first drove west from London to

Bath, the beauty along the roadways calmed and delighted them.

Now, abruptly, the scene changed as they rolled northward through Stratford-upon-Avon and past the industrial blight and dinginess of the great cities of Birmingham and Manchester before reaching the Lake District en route to Scotland's hills.

But, as travelers, they never escaped history. It was everywhere. It was neat and compact on that little island. And they fell in love with the country inns, known until then only by their distant cousins in Virginia and Maryland and West Virginia.

"Brandy, I just had an idea for our list for 'Win'."

"What?"

"Bed and breakfast!"

"Back home?"

"Yes!"

"But, we have that now! I've seen articles in newspapers and interviews and features on TV explaining how more Americans are offering rooms in their homes for tourists."

"I have, too. But there is no grandiose design to it. It's spotty."

"But, it's just starting there."

"I know it is. After what we've seen here so far, just imagine what could be done if 'Win' and some of his business associates made a concerted effort to promote tourist accommodatios in homes rather than skyscrapers!"

"And what do you think the hotel associations would think of that idea, taking business away?"

"Well, hell, they'd probably fight it, but it seems very attractive to me to ween some travelers away from gawdy surroundings and expensive rates to a comfortable home and a chance to meet a real, live American family in Cleveland or Indianapolis or Sacramento, instead of spending a night in a glass and chrome shoebox on the twelfth floor in downtown Detroit!"

"Rog! Don't get so worked up about it!"

"Well, now that I'm thinking about it, I am!"

"We have stayed in some lovely places since we've been here."

"See? Did you like it?"

"Yes, of course. But, over here, it's an adventure and a chance to see the historical places a little more intimately as we travel around."

"Well, don't you think there are plenty of Americans who go to Mount Vernon or Williamsburg or Charlottsville who would feel a little closer to our historical sites if they could meet some people in the area instead of being cooped up in look-alike motels and hotels spread across the country?"

"It is rather boring to see the same prints on the walls! Remember the drive we took down to Miami a few years ago? We had to look out from the hotel windows to fully realize that we were in Fayetteville and Savannah! It's true!"

"Some people like Holiday Inns, I know. And it may fit their particular needs better than a home. But, what would this trip be like if we had stayed at the Stratford-on-Avon Holiday Inn? I can't even imagine it!"

"Rog, it all depends on what a tourist wants."

"That's the point! A traveler should have a choice! In the good old USA we don't have a real choice now. If a couple wanted to stay in a home, they wouldn't have the foggiest where to go. That's where a clearing house would come in for available bed and breakfast places. And, just like us on this trip, we're not in such a big hurry that we wouldn't be willing to drive to an out-of-the-way spot in an area we wanted to see and still have a clean and restful place away from the traffic and congestion of downtown. About all we can do now is call a toll-free number to get a reservation at the next Holiday Inn or Sheraton! Why not make such a service possible for bed and breakfast?"

"I imagine there are people with beautiful homes who have extra rooms and are turned on by meeting people to brighten up their lives and for the extra money."

"In these times, I'll bet there are plenty of them!"

"It would be fun to stay with a family in the Pennsylvania Dutch country or in a home on Jekyll Island, wouldn't it?"

"It would be a hell of a lot more fun than staying in a hotel with a bunch of tourists stomping around overhead or down the halls at all hours!"

"Or businessmen!"

"Jeez, if there is anything I can't stand it's sitting at breakfast in a coffee shop or dining room and listening to some damn salesman at the next table quote prices and company policy to the guy sitting across from him!"

"Do you think it's a practical idea, Rog? Are there enough people out there willing to take overnight guests?"

"Hell, there are here! And besides, that's 'Win's department! They have ways of finding out! Personally, I think this idea is a winner and should be on our list! Leave it to 'Win' to develop it after he determines that it will fly."

"Well, let's keep it in mind. It's a start."

"Hi! How are you feeling today?"

"Better. Much better," Travis said. "They had me walking this morning. Just a while ago. It hurt like hell!"

"It's bound to after an operation. But, they have to get you up on your feet.",

"That nurse Sister Bertha, is so determined!"

"And you must be, too."

"Sweetheart, it was only an appendectomy! You just made it sound as though it is terminal cancer!"

"It was an emergency appendectomy and you know the doctor said it was gangrenous. That was serious enough, darling," Ainsley said, straightening his covers.

"Maybe we should have stayed in Panama instead of coming to San Jose."

"Honey, that wouldn't have made any difference. If it was going to happen, it was going to happen."

"Would you hand me the ice water, sweetheart? I can't quite reach it."

"Want to try to sit up?"

"Pulls too much. Put that straw in it, okay?"

"Did the doctor say when you can leave?"

"Maybe tomorrow, but probably the next."

"I think he looks like Ben Casey, don't you?"

"A Costa Rican Ben Casey! Yes, I guess he does."

"Is this a telegram here?"

"From 'Win'. That guy is sure keeping track of us!"

"Nice. That was sweet of him to send good wishes."

"Well, he does have some money riding on me, too."

"Now, rest a while. I think I'll go back to the hotel and arrange for a ground-level room by the pool. When you get back there, this beautiful weather will fix you up in no time."

"I hope so. I've got to be on my feet and going before too long."

"The most important thing right now is for you to rest and get your strength back."

"I'm not going to let this keep me out of the race. It's going to be a real race now."

"We have plenty of time. You get some rest. I'll be back about five."

"Okay, love."

"Bye, dear."

The flight from Dulles a week earlier brought Travis and Ainsley from muggy Washington to muggy Panama. It was the first trip for either of

them to Central America. Their previous ventures
into the Caribbean area had only taken them as far
as the Bahamas, the first time being soon after
moving to Washington, D.C. Their travel lusts nor-
mally took them to New England or Canada and,
once, to Europe. And chances were good that a special trip now would have taken them back to more
familiar haunts had Travis not been invited to the
convention in Panama City. But, Panama it was.

Thus, their cultural shock was more pronounced
driving from the airport to their hotel in the city. The
poverty was much more than they expected.

"Look at the sugar cane field," Travis said, point-
ing out the window on his side of the taxi.

"How do you know it is?"

"From those white, fuzzy tops on the stalks."

"Learn that in law school?"

"No, I had to do some research on a sugar beet
case, since we've been in Washington, in fact, on
litigation brought by an Idaho firm."

"Smarty!" Ainsley said as she looked up at an old
Panamanian riding down the road on a white horse,
loaded down with a huge woven basket on either side
of its back. The cane tuffs in the field were like a
white chalk line irregularly drawn above the green
plants accenting the rolling green-grassed hills in
the distance. Once past the field, old shack buildings, with an iron-handled water pump outside one
of them, whizzed by. It looked like a scene right out
of the old farm country of their former mid-Western
home.

And, then, they saw a pond with five little kids, at least three naked, who stood in it knee-deep in murky water, and looked at their car as it passed by. And then they saw a girl in the road carrying a ten-gallon tin can, filled with water, on her head. Shanty houses with clothes strung on lines nearby, banana trees in yards, dotted both sides of the road. Closer to the city, the shacks were closer together and the pattern was broken now and then by an inlet with small fishing boats, nets draped on porches of houses to dry or be repaired. Near an old Roman arch bridge were girls and women who bathed and washed clothes in a creek. Here and there, corrugated iron sheets were being hoisted up by men for patches on roofs. Other open fields were green with grass and held small herds of cattle, some under large trees to escape the intense sunlight. And, in the city limits, the large ramshackle, wooden buildings, once used to house laborers during the canal construction days, were still filled to capacity with drying clothes on the railings outside the windows. The taxi driver pointed out those relics which dated to the first of the century. Downtown became more sophisticated with shops, outdoor markets and traffic blocking the streets and intersections. Panama City was noisy and colorful.

Ainsley was happy with their suite in the Hilton with its splendid view of the ocean. She stepped out through the sliding door to the wide balcony and the wonderful, warm breeze caught her hair. Then she came back inside. Travis got on the phone and ordered soda water.

"Are we going to have a drink before dinner?"

"That, Ainsley, is to be used to brush your teeth! I heard Clay talk about it once."

"Even here at the Hilton?"

"Even at the Hilton, dear."

"Good. I'll brush my teeth while you practice your speech!"

Travis picked her up and carried her across the room. "And now I want to tell you about the beds at the Hilton!"

Travis's speech the following night was well-received and politely applauded by nearly 200 delegates at the convention. He and Ainsley sat at the head table decorated with tiny flags of the Americas. The favors at each place setting included bottles of rum, Honduran cigars and orchid corsages for the ladies. The Panamanian delegation came up with beautiful, miniature "keys to the city" charms in tiny, plastic boxes, courtesy of the mayor.

In the course of the reception preceding the dinner, they met the local dignitaries and suave Latinos, many with beautiful wives. The gowns of some of those attending, Ainsley reminded Travis, were elegant and just what she must shop for during their stay. If they weren't available in Panama, she said, she'd be more than willing to go to Rio or Buenos Aires to locate them.

They danced till the new day to the intoxicating Latin rhythm and had great fun, but were up early to take a recommended tour of some of the old colonial fortifications and gardens fronting on the water. The day was bright and, characteristically, the white clouds on the horizon stretched endlessly over the ocean. Huge flowering trees, with pink and red petals bursting from blooms, lined walkways in sweeping parks following the curve of the shore. Old, decayed walls near a four-story fortification tower sprouted green growth, as did the uppermost arched windows, open, now, against the blue sky. Gracefully curved sidewalks invited visitors through the grounds and concrete benches were strategically placed for rest and reflection. Low, stone retaining walls surrounded beautiful, sculpted gardens of exotic plantings and, at one outstanding spot, a Panamanian manicured the beds and lawn. Travis took a picture here, across the garden, laced with brown ground cover and green grass, while his background was palm trees, ferns and deep, red-leafed bushes nestled by a partially fallen wall of stonework, with a single, round window left at the top. He figured it would win a prize for composition in any camera club and it would certainly be a memorable scene to recall their stay in Panama.

Travis bought himself a short-sleeved, stitched Panamanian shirt, the kind worn outside pants, with four pockets and lots of unnecessary buttons, and for Ainsley a pair of walking shoes and the hat he'd promised her. It was a genuine Panama hat, made in Ecuador, with such finely woven material that the clerk passed it through his finger ring to demonstrate the flexibility and quality of its braids. They went to their room, left some of the purchases and put some of them on.

"I love the hat," Ainsley said. "It's so fine and soft."

"Put it on, dear, because we're going flying!"

"What?"

"I read in a brochure on the desk about the San Blas Islands. We can get a little plane and a pilot to fly us over. Want to?"

"Why not! What else do I need?"

"Nothing. Let's go!"

They jumped into a taxi and went to a nearby airport named in the advertisement. At the office in the hangar, they were told it would be about a thirty minute flight. They could look around one of the islands, buy some trinkets and handmade items and spend an hour or so before the hop back.

At the small, green and white painted plane, Travis noticed the name Skywagen stenciled on the side.

"Any parachutes?" he asked the pilot.

"Señor, we don't need them. If the motor stops we glide for miles. A big wing."

They climbed into the back seat and the pilot swung into a front seat and slammed the door. The single-prop motor kicked over and, after giving it plenty of throttle a time or two, the pilot taxied out to the runway.

"Scared?" Travis shouted over the roar.

"A little," Ainsley yelled, and grabbed tightly onto his arm.

The powerful little plane lifted quickly, turned and maybe got up a couple of thousand feet. The green fields, with brown farm houses, made quilt-like patterns and then tangled, green jungle appeared, with reddish soil peeking through here and there. The jungle extended to the water's edge, and looked like a thick shag rug pushed up to a swimming pool. And then they were over the Caribbean.

Shortly, they got their first glimpse of the islands, like potted plants floating on the water. Closer some were so small they only had a dozen or so palm trees jutting up, but surrounded, as all of them were, by a ring of white sand and various shades of green and blue water further out. In the sun, they were like emeralds on the water.

Flying lower, they passed directly over one, with stilt houses visible on the edges, the whole island not more than a block each way. Then they saw grass huts and some wooden pre-fabs painted white, and one green, with flat roofs.

Suddenly, they banked and were headed down toward another, its grassy landing strip bordered on one side by palm trees, on one end of the island. For being unscraped, it wasn't too rough a landing. Motor off, the pilot helped them down and walked with them toward the first houses. A young child, in a sunsuit, with a wide, flat gold cross on a chain around her neck, ran out to meet them. Then, three ladies appeared, one carrying a green parrot on her wrist. They were Cuna Indians, long-time inhabitants of this archipelago. They wore black skirts with varied gold prints woven into them and the distinctive and famous mola tops. The mola designs are stitched on red material and depicted animals, fish, even TV commercials, like Coke, for example. Ainsley noticed the gathered short sleeves and, especially, the gold jewelry with which all were laden. And the nose rings, about the size of a quarter. The necklaces, in multiple strands, were of gold and turquoise. Their heads were covered with scarves and one woman carried a small baby.

The pilot led his passengers about the island to various buildings where items were displayed for sale. They bought four molas. They enjoyed the picture-taking and watched the fishermen and boat building on other parts of the island. The serenity was wonderful and the inhabitants smiled at them. Quite unexpectedly, the pilot introduced them to a Peace Corps volunteer from Vermont, an attractive girl who had been on the islands for a year.

When the small plane rolled down the bumpy strip, lifted and circled widely, gaining altitude, the miniature islands slowly were left behind, as Travis snapped pictures as long as he could.

Panama, in their eyes, turned out to be a fascinating place. The weather wasn't bothering them now and there were plenty of gentle breezes to stave off the mugginess they first experienced. They even created a little breeze of their own by moving about the country. Their transcontinental train ride, albeit forty-nine miles, gave them a look at the Panama Canal as they passed the Gatun Locks and photographed the historical white building, with its red-tiled roof, housing the controls. The date, 1913, was affixed to the building under the name of the locks. From the train, they could see ships that passed through the canal and still be very near the green hills of the countryside. Cranes and other mechanical equipment were alongside the locks of the canal, an engineering miracle that allowed ships their passage across the quiet, little country. They learned that the larger ships were pulled through the canal by small, but powerful, electric locomotives, called mules, on tracks, on either side of the waterway. The Miraflores Locks, at the end nearest Panama City, were of special interest. It was there that they saw a U.S. Navy ship, with white numerals 722 on the gray bow, pass through. The officers were on the bridge of the LST 722, so close one could almost reach out and touch the ship's side. Sailors were seen on the immaculate deck and signal flags flew from the mast. One after another, the ships paraded, foreign registries and names of many countries on their sterns.

The countryside, too, with fields often dotted here and there with sentinel, grotesquely shaped trees, caught their eyes. On the trunk and branches, outlandishly colored orchids often grew and were the parasite, the beautiful, wild pest, as locals called them. These scenes, coupled with visits to government buildings, museums, cathedrals and their daily encounters with Panamanians on the streets and in the shops, enhanced their delight in Panama.

"Like to skip over to the next little country?" Travis asked.

"Costa Rica?"

"Yeah. Let's go to San Jose."

"What do we have for 'Win'? Should we leave now?"

"Well, we've been here about a week and my pockets aren't bulging with treasure to put on the list. Maybe we'll luck out in Costa Rica."

"Have we been on a sharp enough lookout for something?"

"Sweet, we've looked. I don't think we've found."

"Do you think Clay and Rog are having any luck?"

"Honey, we just won't know till we get back."

"I'd be sick to leave tomorrow and think we've overlooked something of interest here."

"I think if we had found something, we'd know it by now."

"Guess you're right. Sure, so let's go."

"You start packing and I'll call the airline."

"Do you think gold nose rings are marketable?"

They immediately fell in love with Costa Rica. Surrounded by the happy, handsome Costa Rican people in a nation without an army, the fabulous climate, the green, lush countryside, where fence posts thrust into the ground sprouted, to walk in the city parks, to feel the excitement of standing on the rim of Irazu, an active volcano 11,260 feet high, and eagerly seeking new sights made their first two days high adventure. Surely their list would begin here.

And, then, they visited the university and, while walking on the campus in the morning sun, Travis doubled up, sat on the grass and was rushed to a Catholic clinic's emergency room.

In the three days since being discharged from the hospital, Travis had quickly regained his strength and had become deeply tanned by hours of sitting by the pool. But he still remembered the first day back at the hotel and those two steps he took on every step of the stairs, both up and down, from their room facing the sun-drenched retreat. And, too, he remembered how he felt anew the pull of the stitches on his abdomen when he quickened his walking gait on the morning they joined other guests in evacuating the hotel when the earthquake struck.

It seemed like everyone in the hotel reached the lobby of the four-story hotel at the same time. It looked like a crowded pack of people just exiting a play on the final curtain at the theater or a movie house emptying while credits rolled.

FIVE

In the Cathay Pacific 707 awaiting departure for
Seoul, via Taipei on Taiwan, Clay glanced at the map
in the seat pocket in front of him and was pleased
that their route would take them over the East
China Sea and the Yellow Sea. That would make
them more than just names on a map. Once airborne
and flying north, huge mainland China, The People's
Republic of China, was far below on his left.

It wasn't long before he saw "little China," Taiwan, on his right and it seemed very small indeed.
From the aircraft, Taiwan looked as flat as a skip-
per-rock.

He had ordered scotch on the rocks just after take off from Hong Kong and hoped it would help to smooth out the flight. He was curled around the pull-down serving table in front of him like a pretzel. It was one, damn dinky seat. He couldn't move anything except his right hand that held his drink. It was a fact of travel overseas and those who flew knew the limited space allotted a passenger in tourist class. Had he been left-handed, he'd have gone thirsty. As it was, the cheap scotch was strong and he felt half-bombed halfway through the small glass. Just as well, for the two Korean ladies that sat next to him on the aisle had proceeded to apply to their noses and cheeks a mentholatum-camphor something or other again, just as they did before take off. He didn't know what it did for them, but it sure cleared out Clay's head as he inhaled the pungent, medicinal fumes. They then produced a small vial of colorless, water-looking "stuff" and liberally sprinkled it down their respective bosoms. Clay had no notion what that was for. Perhaps only ladies knew.

Clay didn't deplane at the brief stop in Taipei, perhaps, in part, because his seatmates made no sign that they would budge their considerable girths. The 707 was up and headed north again and Clay had no chance to change his mind.

The East China Sea and unseen Shanghai slipped by below and soon the Yellow Sea he saw wasn't that at all, for it was, indeed, blue.

And, soon, he saw the Southern end of the Korean peninsula and the plane landed near a huge red pagoda adjacent to the airport. Clay snapped a picture of it when the two Korean ladies preceded him down the aisle.

Surely, he thought, in both ancient and modern Korea, there would be something of interest to discover for the quest. Since it was highly unlikely that either Rog or Travis would venture to this part of the world, he felt it may give him something of an advantage in the race. While he had no idea where either had or not gone outside the States, he could only make the assumption that he wouldn't run into them as he ventured on in the mystical Orient.

His flight was met by Glen, an old Washington friend, who had a driver and car standing by from the American Embassy. Glen Swift was then the Deputy Chief of Mission, the DCM, in Seoul and had served with Clay early on in his career in Washington and Africa. The driver got Clay's bags, unopened by customs agents, as a courtesy usually extended to foreign representatives traveling abroad on a Diplomatic Passport. As a general rule, other government employees who carried Official Passports were also seldom searched as they entered a foreign country. That rule was often negated, however, when entering a nation under certain sanctions by the United States and, too, especially the USSR, before the fall of the communistic government there, and in other East Bloc nations in their orbit. Americans found Russia fitful to enter, and leave, because of their stringent customs rules and baggage searches, even to strip-searches, which were not unusual.

"What a treat, Glen, to see you after a number of years! Congratulations on your assignment here in Korea."

"When we received a cable from Washington on your travel schedule, I really looked forward to your visit. Welcome, old pal, to Seoul."

"I'm glad my first visit here found you in the higher reaches of the embassy. Really good to see you!" Then Clay added, "I really always hated to have my luggage rifled. Thanks. It's a bore."

"Well, let's get you to your hotel so you can rest up a bit."

"An army compound, I understand?"

"The New Naija Hotel, right around the corner from The Naija Hotel, which is the R&R for U.S. military in Korea. You can almost believe you'll run into M*A*S*H's Hawkeye and B.J. there!"

At the New Naija Hotel, Clay had a twelfth or top floor room, small, but with a view of some nearby jagged hills that formed a backdrop for the city. But, of course, after Hong Kong, Seoul seemed drab. It's industrial capacity, however, had been stirred to a fever pitch since the Korean War and South Korea became an economic power in the region, the nearness of North Korea notwithstanding.

In some very obvious aspects, however, its underdevelopment was glaring. Take Clay's room, for instance: he was shocked to see a coil of rope near the only window. It was his fire escape! There was a metal gripper handle attached to the rope to allow one to slide down the outside of the hotel without getting rope burn on the hands. But, Great Caesar,

Clay thought, he could hardly see himself tossing that rope out, twelve stories high, and climbing over the window sill, for a slide to safety! The "rope trick," as he began to think of it, would not pass the test for an item to take back to Delaware on his list in the quest. It was a lifeline of sorts, true, but rather remote to even faintly imagine that it would command usage anywhere in the States. A young man or woman may have been able to use such an escape venture, but what about the elderly or the infirm? What about children?

Then the idea struck Clay as he sat on the edge of his bed and fixed his gaze on that coiled rope: some years earlier he had visited Russia, Moscow and Leningrad more specifically, and he noted then, with great interest, that the new, grand hotels where Americans and other foreigners were usually lodged, had an item worthy of his short list for "Win" in the quest: it was "a fact" that he saw with his own eyes in amazement, that each and every room had a small glass-fronted cabinet on a wall that held smoke masks! Yes! Smoke masks or hoods with goggle-like spectacles for protecting the eyes and they looked as if they'd be so easy to access and pull over your head as you made your way in a fire, through thick smoke that usually kills many victims in hotels over the world, to possible safety in getting to stairways in such a horrid emergency. Clay stood up and slapped his hands together in excitement.

Yes! "Win" had placed no restrictions on the "when" and "where" worthy objects for the list may have been found. None!

"Great Caesar!" he exclaimed aloud.

The smoke hood was a must and a first for his list, he decided. The hood was so obviously a great idea it was a wonder that travelers to the USSR hadn't brought the idea back to the States and sold Congress or hotel chains on the idea. Even commercial buildings and private homes. At least Clay had heard of no such result. He thought of hotel fires in Las Vegas and even the terrorist bombing of the New York Trade Center where many were felled for lack of smoke protectors in dire building fires' emergencies. He reasoned that surely he wasn't the first to think of the smoke hoods as life savers. Maybe it was the Russian hotel builders or maybe the idea originated in another part of the world and incorporated by the Russians as a safety feature of their own hotels. Whatever the derivation, Clay determined then and there in his twelfth floor room at the New Naija Hotel that the smoke hoods idea would head his list, unless, of course, he came upon an item of even greater potential. But, at the moment, he could think of nothing that could be employed so quickly and economically that its marketability would surely be a fantastic success. Perhaps he could learn via legal channels in Washington, D.C., whether such a patent for a smoke hood was on record and whether it was employed anywhere in the States.

Clay was ecstatic. Why, he wondered, had it taken him so long, so very long, to reach back a few years into memory to recall those smoke hoods! Yes! It was the rope! That innocent, but frightening, coil of rope only a few feet from him by his lone window.

That had triggered it: it brought forth an idea as an alternative to, perhaps, sure death were he called upon to toss that pile of hemp out that window only to fall in terror to the street below if fire engulfed the hotel and he failed to hold onto that flimsy handle on the escape rope, the only way to safety.

He grabbed the room key on the low dresser, took the elevator to the lobby and rounded the corner on the street to get to the Naija Hotel. He found the bar off the small lobby and quickly ordered a scotch and water. His mouth was dry from his recent thoughts. The hotel accepted only U.S. money so he had tossed his leftover Hong Kong dollars into his briefcase in his hotel room. As he took his glass in hand, he was sure that it must have been the thought of fire that so parched his throat. The bartender smiled at him as he saw Clay relax his facial muscles. Little did he know what had caused Clay's calm composure to return. It was more the satisfying thought of finding a wonderful idea deep in his mind than the soothing flavor of the Johnnie Walker liquid, Red Label, on his tongue and throat.

The embassy people had lined up three dinners and two lunches for Clay in the three days he'd be in Seoul. Meetings were held with embassy staff as well as high Korean government officials on a host of topics. Clay had looked at the figures of the Korean program and met with several of the key per-

sonnel on the economic side of things as well as the
political. It was somewhat difficult to keep general
conversations in focus when the contrasts between
Hong Kong and Seoul crept into his thoughts. Everything after the bustling British colony was downhill
and Clay found South Korea's capital drab. He was
driven through the city a number of times and was
struck, however, by the broadness of the streets and
the many modern buildings near the local landmark,
the East Gate. At Youngson, the U.S. Army base, he
was walked through the commissary and the post-
exchange and later saw an American compound of
government housing. Many subjects and sights in a
short period of time tended to cause confusion rather
than understanding. But, when someone from Washington visited, it seemed that everyone wanted to be
in on endless meetings and hoped to press the visitor
with personal and staff problems. Clay almost
wanted the days to end so that he could more leisurely enjoy his evenings.

On a particular drive back to his hotel after a
hectic schedule, the full moon looked spectacularly
beautiful, cold and lonesome over Seoul. The night
was clear and very chilly.

A Sunday evening buffet at the Officers' Club at
the Youngson base was very pleasant. Clay even
succeeded in getting a well-done end cut of beef as a
ten-piece Korean orchestra, decked out in tuxedos,
played U.S.-style dinner music on a little stage at
one side of the dining room.

Once back in his hotel room, a single-bulb ceiling
light trying its best to brighten the room, Clay locked

the door. But, as in so many places he'd stayed on
out-of-Washington trips, there was no chain or
deadbolt on the door. He had first noticed it when he
checked in. He always felt half-naked in a strange
hotel, large or small, where he couldn't really depend
on his personal safety and privacy. Of two things he
was sure at that hotel: an intruder could easily pick
the single lock; and could enter his room as he slept
from the window, if he came off the roof. There were
no fire escape stairs, only that damn coil of rope.
Well, and besides, he thought, who in hell would
want to come in and get him? He always avoided
street level rooms, but, now, on the twelfth floor of
that hotel, he cringed at the thought of playing
Spider-Man on the outside wall to escape anyone.

Next morning, another schedule of briefings and
interviews was developed at the embassy. He took
comfort in the fact that he was at the heart of one of
the most successful economic development programs
in the world. And, even more happily, word came to
him that a trip for him was to be arranged to the
compound at the North-South border, the famed
DMZ (Demilitarized Zone) near the 38th Parallel.
He was really excited about Panmunjom should the
trip materialize: a strip of land 151 miles long and
2-1/2 miles wide was a shield for freedom.

Later in the day, Clay was told that a North-
South meeting was scheduled at the 38th and tours
to the compound were cancelled.

Among the many rumors that generally flew
over North Korea and South Korea, one was that the
United Nations had been invited to see the tunnels

constructed by the North under a part of the South's defenses. Great Caesar! Clay was appalled that such an underground honeycomb could be built without swift detection. The news of the tunnels, unusual meetings between the North and South, not too common, and Clay's lost chance to see a pivotal point of Far East history was painful for the trip there was looked upon by him as the icing on the cake of a unique experience, a once in a lifetime opportunity available to few. The tunnels were worldwide, sensational news and had Clay been able to see and tour them, he felt sure that a second event such as that would find a place for "Win"'s list in good stead along with the smoke hoods. But it was not to be.

A few walks on sun-drenched streets in Seoul made the city take on a brighter character in Clay's mind in contrast to that first impression. Even his disappointment over the trip to the border was lightened. And the smoke hoods! The secret of the hoods remained locked in his mind to cheer him when boring meetings or visits to sites of note got him down. What a jewel! What a find! What a remembrance that so suddenly came back to him from a trip to Russia! And another unbelievable fact now and then crept into his remembrances of Moscow: the long brick walls that surround the Kremlin, and the spectacular view of them from Red Square, were built when Columbus discovered America! To behold them and try to think back to the 1490's, over 500 years ago, was nearly unfathomable. How very new was our America as a nation. And now, Korea, all of it, makes the old USSR seem like a very young pup.

An evening was arranged to attend a Kisaeng dinner. Clay was told that nearly every official visitor to Korea, even members of Congress, go to them as a traditional type of entertainment.

Clay's dinner party was made up of both embassy personnel and Koreans from the private sector, about eight in all. There was no briefing as to what to expect, but Clay imagined it may be the Korean version of Japan's geisha girls to entertain men.

The two embassy cars drove to an establishment in a good neighborhood, it seemed, and were ushered into a large private dining room beautifully decorated and featured a mammoth, low rectangular table, highly polished, around which the men were seated on cushions.

They had left their shoes in a hallway and slipped on soft, cloth sandals. Clay found it relatively comfortable to sit cross-legged by the table. Two waitresses poured small cups of tea as the easy conversation of their group commenced.

Shortly, each man was introduced to a beautifully robed dinner companion, who entered the dining room ever so quietly, and all were young women with pleasant smiles on their made-up faces. They placed napkins on the men's laps and poured more tea, which soon gave way to wine and, finally, to quart bottles of Johnnie Walker Red Label Scotch. Clay thought himself fortunate that it was his brand

and not some less palatable variety. Each person, sixteen now, drank from small, stemmed silver wine glasses which held at least a generous jigger of beverage at a filling. When a cup was raised in a toast to anyone at the table, all drank the cupful. Early on in the evening, it seemed as though each of them had toasted all around the table and to some, twice or three times.

When the steaming, varied dishes of dinner were served, their companions assisted them in selections and kept their plates brimming with Korean delicacies of meat, fish, vegetables and rice.

And the toasts, with the Red Label Scotch, continued sporadically, throughout the meal: toasts to countries, to people, to programs, to their hostesses and to the hosted.

When the table was cleared, they got back to a good wine and, then, quite unexpectedly to Clay, each girl, in turn, modestly exposed a breast and tipped her stemmed, small glass over a nipple of soft, delicate skin. Each man, also in turn around the table, savored the wine as he licked it from his companion's breast.

And, then, it was the men's turn, while it was obvious that Koreans, perhaps all Orientals, as far as Clay knew, took pride in body hairlessness. There were giggles all around the table as the men, one by one, unbuttoned their shirts. The Americans especially, Clay included, got the biggest laughs, but their companions were not hesitant in their part of tasting of the fine wine, each couple now having participated twice in the company of the others.

Clay suddenly thought: Great Caesar! What an icebreaker this little ritual would be, yes, this daring gambit, at some of those stodgy party/cocktail circuits he well-knew in Washington, D.C.! It would doubtlessly cause even more of a sensation than those see-through blouses worn at such functions of yesteryear by some Senate and diplomats' wives and would even eclipse the women's fashions of late to go braless and to wear deeply-slit tops of evening gowns to high society dinner parties.

As general drinking continued, and a small string instrument group appeared on a small stage, the guests were encouraged to go up to a microphone and sing American, well-known songs. Clay didn't remember walking toward the stage when his turn came and, he may have even crawled. He knew the words to the song being played for him, but words didn't come out right. But, no matter, it was an attempt in the glow of camaraderie.

Whether by design or happenstance, Clay's lovely companion of the previous evening was at his side as the first bright rays of the Korean sunrise, that slowly climbed over the nearby jagged rocky foothills, cut a warm swath into his hotel room. Her silk robe had been replaced by a simple white blouse and a pair of washed, so-American, blue jeans, now draped haphazardly over a straight-backed chair in the room.

Clay was up, shaved and showered and dressed as she stood under the warm water and washed her long, black hair. Then, quickly, she put on her only two pieces of clothing and slipped her feet, with red painted nails, into heelless slip-ons of straw.

They took a taxi at Clay's hotel and he got out at the American Embassy and she went her way somewhere in Seoul.

It wasn't until much later in the day that Clay recalled parts of the dinner as a very unique and sensual experience, delicate and beautiful. He didn't remember the rest at all.

At his meeting at the Ministry of Finance, Clay was impressed by the manner and deep concerns of the gentleman who gave him some twenty minutes of his time. First-off, he spoke of Korea's wood needs. He discussed the involvement and commitment of the Korean people in the development of their country. He said they were achieving their goals. Clay spoke of his Latin American experience where he had seen so many examples of self-help and intense interest of the people in getting on with the economic development of their countries and need to decrease their dependence on outside assistance. At the end, Clay assured him that he would probably be an unofficial spokesman on behalf of the spirit of the Korean people in modernizing and developing their nation.

On Clay's walk to a luncheon meeting, the dozens of young, uniformed school children, neatly dressed, combed and polished, that he encountered on the streets, bore out the fruits of educational advances and the emphasis on excellence the Korean official had stressed.

That night, Clay went to a stag dinner at Glen Swift's home. There were nine. The house was tastefully furnished and was filled with items collected from years of travel throughout the world. Served with white and red wine, they enjoyed chicken pie, pre-boned Korean trout, with both head and tail, beef, peas and mushrooms, fried potatoes, cheeses and pie, capped with champagne. During the stimulating conversation at and following dinner, the host, at one point, gave Clay a small brass snail piece from his living room coffee table, when Clay spoke of shopping for a typical Korean brass object.

"Just as the Arabs do," Glen said, "you admire; you get." It was a relaxing and pleasant evening and Clay was pleased to learn of Glen's travels and family.

Next morning, the embassy staff sent Clay's plane tickets, passport and luggage out ahead to the airport to avoid the crush. It was a slightly overcast day and Clay knew he'd miss those crisp mornings and evenings in Manila, his next destination. Everyone warned him to prepare for the blast of heat.

Clay got his last look at Seoul en route to the airport. He liked the wide streets and their cleanliness. And the bright, black-uniformed school kids, with bulging briefcases.

And, he certainly wouldn't miss that damn rope in his room nor the magical way it brought to his mind those smoke hoods in old Russia that still held first place on his unwritten list for the quest.

At the Northwest Airlines ticket counter, an embassy staff member met Clay with his tickets, passport and luggage checks and he was ushered to a nearby VIP lounge to await boarding time. When the staffer departed, Clay was alone in the well-decorated room, home-like, with cold beverages in view, some good magazines and comfortable chairs. He picked up a copy of TIME, removed his jacket and sat down in a Scan lounger with a matching ottoman.

Unexpectedly, there was a sudden knock on the door.

"Come in," said Clay, who remained seated, the magazine on his lap.

Two men in trenchcoats, looking every bit like the typical police detectives in movie spy stories, entered and closed the door.

"Mr. Stevenson?" one asked.

"Yes," Clay responded.

"Mr. Clay Stevenson?"

"I am. What is this about?"

"May I see your passport, sir?" one asked.

Clay got up, walked to the chair on which he had hung his suit jacket, removed his passport from the inside breast pocket and handed it to the taller of the two men who had asked for it.

"Thank you, Mr. Stevenson," he said, looked at the picture in the Diplomatic Passport and then directly at Clay.

"Who are you?" Clay now asked.

"Interpol, Mr. Stevenson. I'm O'Brien," he said as he flashed his identity card in its leather wallet. "This is Max Smith, my associate." Both wallets had photos.

"What is it you want?" Clay said, as he remained standing.

"We just have a few questions, Mr. Stevenson."

About what, Clay wondered: his departure for Manila, the Kisaeng dinner, the purpose of his few days in Seoul, the conference in Hong Kong?

"It is about the Tiptons, Mr. Stevenson, a Bruce and an Anne Tipton. You are acquainted with them?"

"Slightly. Only slightly. Can we talk here? Is this a proper place, this VIP lounge, for an interrogation?" He didn't know it had been electronically "swept" by an Interpol crew an hour earlier.

"We only have a few questions. This room is fine, just fine. Please continue about the Tiptons."

"I met them on the flight from the U.S. to Tokyo and they later came to Hong Kong. We met, went to dinner, as I recall. Maybe lunch. Mr. Tipton, Bruce, is a patent attorney out of Washington, D.C., and an acquaintance of a friend of mine, Travis Goodson."

"And..."

"And, what? We said our goodbyes at the Hong Kong Hilton and we went our separate ways."

"May I see into your briefcase, Mr. Stevenson?"

"For what reason? What are you looking for? Just what in the world is all of this about?"

"May we look?"

"Go ahead! It isn't locked," Clay said resignedly.

The taller man watched Clay's eyes while the other man in a trenchcoat opened the briefcase. He moved a few things about and lifted out something wrapped in a small hand towel.

"Am I being searched for a hotel hand towel from Hong Kong?" Clay asked rather heatedly.

"No, Mr. Stevenson. But for what may be wrapped in this towel."

"Damned if I can remember what I wrapped up! Unwrap it and we'll all know!" he said.

"Oh, I think I know what it is," said the tall man. "Smith!"

Smith unrolled the towel to reveal the brass figure the Tiptons gave to Clay in Hong Kong.

"You knew what was in the towel, O'Brien?" Clay asked.

"Oh, yes. We were at the metal detector in this airport when your briefcase was passed through."

"So?"

"So, Mr. Stevenson, we were disappointed that you brought that object out of Seoul in a towel."

"O'Brien, I remind you that I'm an American citizen, an employee of the Department of State in Washington, D.C., and travel, as you have noted, on a Diplomatic Passport. I don't see..."

"We see, Mr. Stevenson. We know all about you. What you obviously don't know is our interest in that brass object."

"It was a gift...from Anne Tipton, as a memento of Hong Kong and..." Clay said.

"Please. Mr. Stevenson, please listen," said the tall one and he turned the bronze statue from side to side and top to bottom.

"Yes, I hear that! I heard it in my Hong Kong Hilton room when I unwrapped that gift from Anne...," Clay said.

"There is something inside...."

"Sure...a piece of brass that may have inadvertently been trapped inside during its manufacture...or..."

"We are fairly certain what is inside, and it is not a waste piece or pieces of brass," the tall one said assertively.

"Then what the hell is it?" Clay now said, lifting his voice.

"It is a priceless jade necklace, of Chinese antiquity that was stolen from the British Government's Colonial Museum in Hong Kong."

"O'Brien, I can assure you that an American diplomat would be highly unlikely to steal, let alone attempt to assist an exit from Hong Kong..."

"Oh, Mr. Stevenson, I beg to differ with you. An American embassy or Department official of rank, such as yourself, would be the perfect foil to evade detection."

"If you suspect that I would..."

"It is not what we suspect, Mr. Stevenson, it is what we know."

Great Caesar! Clay thought. Could the Tiptons have played him for a courier to exit Hong Kong with a stolen rare necklace of jade?

"I trusted the Tiptons, O'Brien, to..."

"In this part of the world, Mr. Stevenson, trust only goes as far as the border guards. We allowed you to depart Hong Kong to Seoul, remain the few days there, and thence to this airport to see if the Tiptons would try to contact you to retrieve the brass piece on some pretense or another. They did not. And we have just learned here at the Seoul Airport, before approaching you in this VIP lounge, that the Tiptons were detained several hours ago and corroborated your account as just given to us. They are in a lounge, similar to this one you are in, but a hundred yards away. They have been placed under arrest by the Seoul police at our request and, upon the removal of the jade necklace from the brass Buddha, they will be formally charged with grand theft by Hong Kong authorities and you, Mr. Stevenson, will be free to continue your itinerary to Manila and other points in the Orient."

"Great Caesar! The Tiptons!" Clay exclaimed. He sat down in the Scan and stretched out his legs on the ottoman to relax.

"Now, Mr. Stevenson, you are aware that trained eyes can plainly see the obvious use of an acetylene torch flame to remove the bottom from your "gift" brass piece, insert the jade necklace and even some assorted rare Chinese coins, as from the Hong Kong museum, inside the hollow figure, and hope to have them delivered, via you, to a place they could reclaim the cache, perhaps in a very undignified manner, yes, perhaps taking your life, to secure a fortune via a jewel fence in America."

"I had no idea...I heard the clunk...that..."

"Our experts," said the tall one, "will remove the ancient pieces, replace the bottom of brass and will be happy to forward your Mi-Lo Fo Buddha to the Department of State in Washington D.C. You will never see a blemish on the piece when you display it in your home or office. And, Mr. Stevenson, we thank you for your cooperation. We have the Tiptons, just down the hall, we have the museum pieces..."

"O'Brien, how do you know I didn't switch the Buddhas, you have the one with the brass clunkers inside and I have the one with jade and coins?" Clay said in jest.

"Clever, but, Mr. Stevenson, we know only one Buddha was sold at the China Fleet Club in Hong Kong in the past month and that was this particular one the Tiptons bought."

"Marked in some way, no doubt."

"Here is the mark, here by my thumb. Can you see it?" said the tall one.

"Plain as the nose on..."

"And, Mr. Stevenson, would you like to consider a tip should you decide to purchase an item of jade for your wife...or a friend...?"

"Of course."

"A mean test as to a quality jade piece is really very simple: place or rub the jade at the side of your nose. The colder it feels, the more valuable it is. And, of course, there are other tests, much more refined by dealers and miners of jade that are employed to determine value, but the "nose" test is quite accurate. Try it the next time you encounter some jade, say, the very piece that you can't live without," the tall one said with a smile, his first.

"My plane! I may have missed my plane for Tokyo and Manila!" Clay declared.

"Your plane awaits you, by our request, at the gate assigned. Mr. Smith will accompany you. You see, Interpol business can be as important and demanding as diplomacy. Good-day, Mr. Stevenson, and thank you. Would you like for me to extend your regards to the Tiptons?" the tall one said, facetiously.

Without answering, Clay hurried from the VIP lounge, Smith, in the other trenchcoat, trotting to keep up, with Clay's jacket and briefcase.

SIX

Clay felt frazzled after the chase down the hallways to his plane, trying not to slip on the floors, to
keep an eye on Smith, trudging along with his suit
jacket and briefcase, find the right gate and locate
his seat at the plane's rear, as somewhat angry
stares fell on him from some of the passengers. He
knew he had held up the flight and for how long he
couldn't even guess. He hadn't taken the time to look
at his watch. He almost didn't care after the episode
in the VIP Lounge, O'Brien, the tall, and Smith, the
other, and, to top it off, he felt "used" by the Tiptons.
Damn the Tiptons! he thought. He also had the
distinct feeling that while he'd like to cuff Bruce

Tipton around the ears and gently slap the wrist of
Anne, whom he thought had given him a heartfelt
gift for getting a room for them at the Hong Kong
Hilton, he figured the Hong Kong police would work
them over pretty good by meting out British justice
for those who would steal art treasures from the
Colonial Museum.

As the plane got up and away, Clay ordered a
scotch and water to soften the utter frustration he
felt, not only about the detention by Interpol agents,
and the actions of the Tiptons, but now he discovered
a seatmate, a lady, next to him was from the Seoul
embassy, had heard Clay speak to the staff, and
talked an ear off him starting as he sat down. Great
Caesar! he thought. He seemed to be getting it from
all sides.

He took a sip of scotch as she began her story:
the numerous comments she had heard about Clay's
briefing the other day and Clay wondered, through
her monotone recitation, whether any staff had
noted his shakes and bleary eyes from the night
before; how other staff had told her of Clay's convic-
tion and feeling and compassion for the way to deal
with people-related problems; that she was from
Michigan, had a home on some lake; was going non-
stop from Tokyo to LA, then to Houston to visit a
daughter, and on to Washington, D.C. to participate
in a conference; and that she was in education and
used to teach at Michigan State. At her last words
on other subjects, of absolutely no interest to Clay,
the plane, blessedly, landed and her voice trailed off
as she walked down the corridors in the Tokyo air-

port to catch her flight to LA, as Clay found his gate for Manila in another direction.

There was a scant thirty minutes between planes in Tokyo. Clay made his way to a souvenir shop nearby and bought a small, golden sake cup. Later, it was to remind him more of Seoul than Tokyo.

There were now loading problems before departure and a delay, but Clay was cheered to learn there would be a brief stopover on Okinawa en route to Manila. His new seatmate to Naka City was the Potentate, Aloha Temple, Hawaii, who was on his way to an international exposition there where most of the people on that plane got off. Then it quickly filled up again for Manila.

Clay's mind now wandered to Rog and Travis and he wondered where in the world they might be at that very moment. Clay just sat and thought. He had no idea where they were, nor what they may find, or had already found. Could they have happened upon two outstanding things for each of them? Or, more; or less? Clay now had but one he felt comfortable with: the smoke hoods. He was sure that each of the three men viewed their quest in their own ways. That thought dredged up a story he hadn't thought about in the years since he first heard it: The boss sent two salesmen to a certain country to open up a new shoe market. One wired back: "People don't wear shoes here. I'm catching the next plane home!" The other wired: "Great opportunity here. I'm never coming back!" Well, those were two divergent thoughts for sure. Could Rog and Travis have things figured out in a whole different way than did Clay? There was an old saying, too: struggle and suffering breed character. There was a struggle; there was a contest. Oh, Clay didn't have any way to measure whether he was suffering or not. Maybe he was; maybe he wasn't. Who knew?

Clay's reverie was interrupted as another new passenger stepped on his foot and kicked his brief-case stowed under the seat in front of him as the huge man took a seat next to him. When in hell will this plane be full and take me to Manila? Clay wondered.

Rog and Brandy may be having lunch with Pierre Salinger in Paris right then. And Travis? Could he and Ainsley be the guests of the President of Haiti or Mexico or Brazil? Maybe Rog couldn't get away from the clinic and just stayed home to stew in his own juice. And Travis and Ainsley may have, on the other hand, been captured by bandits in Colombia.

As the plane finally made its run for takeoff, Clay's mind hastened back to Hong Kong and those washed clothes he saw strung around on buildings en route to the New Territories. He could see many bright colors catching breezes and flying like kites. And he thought back, again, to his little Mom and her remark about her own family either being awfully clean or awfully dirty on wash day in his youth.

Then Clay mused that he must have been a vain little snot as a kid because each morning, after washing, dressing, eating breakfast and before going to school, he'd dip his long comb into a tall jar of hair groom, green in color, that had a tad thinner consistency than rubber cement, then carefully parted it and slicked back his blond, straight hair. All day, in school, at play at recess, in after-school street games, like kick the can, or even going roller skating around the neighborhood and, often after a good night's sleep, not a hair had moved out of place. To the touch, his hair felt glued and stiff. Only a good hair wash got the goo out. He lost, over the years, some of his vainness along with some of his hair, no longer worn matted, starched-like, to his scalp. Why he then thought of all that, he had no idea. Maybe he thought a reintroduction of the hair groom product may be marketable, somewhere, and should be on his list for "Win."

How people changed! And the new sounds of the language Clay heard.

Clay was met by an embassy car at midnight at the Manila Airport and the local hire driver chatted freely on the way into the city. Clay's ears were not yet attuned to the lilting, pleasing, Spanish and Portuguese tongues of Latin America, with which he was more familiar, after the Chinese, Japanese and Korean he heard in his earlier surroundings from Hong Kong to Seoul. The driver seemed pleased that the American he had in his car conversed with him in something of a common language. They shared some travel stories and a laugh or two.

At the Bayview Plaza Hotel on Manila Bay, Clay's luggage in the lobby, and his driver gone, he had no reservation and the hotel was filled to capacity. The night clerk, happily, made some calls to nearby hotels and finally located a room at the Manila Hilton for what was left of the night.

Next morning, Clay moved back to the Bayview for the U.S. Embassy was just across the street and from his ninth floor room of the hotel, he had a perfect view of the magnificent bay.

He lunched with some embassy staff at the Swiss Inn, bad service but good food. It was mentioned that Muhammad Ali, known much earlier in his boxing career as Cassius Clay, stayed at the Manila Hilton during his visit some years earlier for his hyped-fight with Joe Frazier in a heavyweight bout that was dubbed the "Thrilla in Manila," one of several Ali-Frazier championship encounters.

After lunch, Clay's driver took him to the post exchange and a brief stop at Tsoro's Gift Shop where he bought some wooden carvings for his Washington staff. A heavy work schedule followed in the embassy.

That evening, he went alone to the Japanese restaurant on the top of his hotel and took a small table by a window overlooking Manila Bay. The view was spectacular. The sunset was brilliant color...and not just one sunset, but many in an ever-changing sky. To look at it was like taking single-frame, slow-motion movies with his eyes. Finally, the sky seemed to fill with black, irregular brush strokes, daubed on a gray background, and impressed him to the point he tried to sketch its dark beauty on a page from his journal of the trip. And then, too soon, it was night, with only the lights of anchored ships reflected on the shimmering water.

With the marvelous distraction gone from view, he listened to some Japanese speakers, both hotel guests and staff, and the true sounds of the Orient were heard anew.

And, then, he knew he must focus on what the trip was all about. First, it was a working trip. Long conference hours and sessions in Seoul attested to that. And there would be much more. Only secondly, could he devote some free time to the equally serious business of the scavenger hunt. But, thus far on the trip, it had been difficult to maintain those priorities. It seemed as though he was continually thinking about what he was looking for to bring back for the confrontation with Travis and Rog. To rationalize, he thought for a while that maybe he had stored up some information unconsciously, and maybe even had some new objects packed in his luggage then that would merit presentation in the game. But, yet, it didn't really seem so and, perhaps, he was just fooling himself. Maybe, in fact, he was fooling away a hundred opportunities and didn't realize it. Maybe that dice game he watched on the flight from Dulles Airport to LA was a candidate for his list. Most, if not all people, liked games of one kind or another. Perhaps not dice games, but card games and party games, and it would be very difficult to hit upon something new that would catch the public's fancy. However, many people were hooked on one or several sports: tennis, golf, soccer, football, basketball, baseball, auto racing, horse or dog racing, hockey as participants or, more likely, as spectators. Clay's thoughts turned even to something as versatile as the soy bean...or the peanut shell of an earlier era...something in abundance that may now be wasted or shunned but could be transformed and utilized or put to work in a whole new form...just as the soy bean and the lowly peanut shell became important derivatives. He smiled as he thought: if people buy pet rocks, hoola hoops, Barbies, commemorative stamps, like the Marilyn Monroe and the Elvis, T-shirts, Levi's, Elmo...why wouldn't they buy....what?

The time seemed to be getting away from Clay, too. Hong Kong, Seoul, Manila and then Jakarta, Bangkok on urgent embassy business, his secret mission included, every day on a flight or in a meeting, as the thirty he began with in Washington, dwindled down to a precious few. It was hard to work and play a game, trying to do a good job at both, when you're in a race with time.

The game goes on. The game goes on and on.

Next morning, Clay remembered people's voices in the lobby, the elevator, the restaurant and on television. What a difference there was in the sounds of places and peoples. Only a few days earlier, the Chinese, the Japanese, the Korean language speakers were dominant but had all slightly faded and, once again, some Spanish, and Tagalog, the national language of the Philippines, had caught up with him. He felt that he was back in the Western Hemisphere and that the Philippines had been misplaced in the Orient. Maybe that is why he was anxious to leave for Jakarta in Indonesia and hurry back to the Far East and the vocal sounds he was eager to hear again. He knew, in his mind, he was anxious to separate the two into their proper geographic spheres. Early Spanish explorations in the Philippine islands' chain had left their mark in the peoples' language, even in the midst of the more predominate ethnic groups in the area of Manila.

The embassy people in Seoul were so right: the heat in Manila could be stifling and while blue skies and white clouds were evident, a smoky haze hung just above all the downtown buildings and seemed intent on inhibiting a good, decent breath of air and only increased one's discomfort in such a warm clime.

When the electricity in the embassy cut off for three hours, the temperature rose to near ninety degrees. It only affected a part of the embassy and Clay's office was in that area. His jacket came off and he was wringing wet. A fan helped minimally, a small one with batteries. Now, there is an idea, Clay thought, as the tiny blade moved the humid air with some success. Outside, there was precious little breeze but the ugly smog had now disappeared. Clay could see for miles across the city.

During a part of his office day, a staffer advised Clay that the French and Russian restaurants in Singapore were quality eateries. Singapore would be one stopover on the flight to Jakarta and Clay hoped his two hours there would be interesting for he planned to go to the famed Raffles Hotel for tea in the lobby!

His last evening in Manila found him at the Japanese restaurant atop his hotel and one more sunset with his scotch and water. He would be taking a staff car to the home of a military attache in the embassy for a send-off dinner.

Conversation that evening was rather boring: some had property in Montana, all played their share of golf, enjoyed cruises, two had lived together and finally got married, many knew "the swingers" of the "old" crowd and didn't know where to retire. Clay entertained them with his sand collection stories and his letters to the editor printed in The New York Times, The Wall Street Journal, The Washington Post and others in which Clay found delight in finding some "news" stories humorous, and editors seemed to be on the lookout for short, punchy letters on subjects of the day. They felt that people needed a bit of relief from the barrage of stories, mostly morbid, that filled newspapers and Clay had compiled a book, smallish, of his letters published over several decades. It was a hobby. Some of his letters drew death threats, like when the farmers closed down Washington, D.C. traffic with huge tractors from around the country. Clay still had those letters somewhere in his den in Georgetown. And, yes, they were a bit spooky to receive over a light piece he'd written for The Washington Post. He had a copy of that letter in his pocket that found its way around the dinner table:

"Yippee! I tip my Stetson to the Metropolitan Police Department for their successful annual round-up of those pesky tractor critters Feb. 5. Our boys just fenced in that stampedin' herd that ran rampant through our town the other morn. All us commuters were mighty grateful to see those mavericks hobbled for a spell.

"Now, I ain't for brandin' or breakin' or hobblin', for that matter, but boys, we got to git this place back to like Home on the Range. A body gits tired of this discouragin' stuff."

Next morning, Clay got a glimpse of Corregidor Island at the entrance to Manila Bay as the Captain reported it to passengers on the flight south to Jakarta via Singapore. The weather was near perfect and Clay began to settle down after the usual airport exercise. He wished the whole thing could be computerized some way. People dislike an upset stomach at every airport encounter and maybe the problem could be solved if passengers could just get on a conveyor belt and move right to the plane like the luggage.

It would be a three hour flight to Singapore, like from National Airport in D.C. to Denver, only more exotic because of some place names involved and, too, those far away places most never reach.

At the Singapore Airport, Clay had a beer, Anchor by name, and walked about a bit during the two hour lay over. He was fascinated by the beautiful islands below as his plane landed in Singapore. After the Jakarta visit, he would pass through Singapore again en route to Bangkok and may try the Russian Troika restaurant there should time allow. And, he'd have to wait until after Jakarta, for sure, to go to the Raffles Hotel. There was just not time enough in two hours to do what he planned.

SEVEN

"The palace of THAT Henry,
Who did, with girls, cavort!
For us, 'twas a lasting highlight,
They call it Hampton Court.

"We did it all quite proper,

As tourists, not at all,
Though driving on the left-hand side,
Nor faithful car to stall."

Rog finished the reading of the latest install-
ment of his epic poem to chronicle the European trip.
He was seated on the bed, a pillow at his back, his
shoes on the floor and a gin on the rocks in his hand.
His suit jacket was on a nearby chair.

"Well, what do you think?" he asked Brandy.

"What was that last line?"

"Well, it was, 'Nor faithful car to stall.'"

"Oh."

"'Oh?'" Rog asked. "Does that 'Oh' mean the line
is too gargled, doesn't rhyme properly or what?"

"It means just what I said, 'Oh.'"

"You hate the line."

"I didn't say that."

"You think I should give it some more thought
and change it."

"I didn't say that," Brandy said.

"You think that maybe to say that the faithful
car hasn't stalled will be a bad omen, bad luck, and
that it might stall when we head out in the morning?"

"Oh, no, Rog. The car will be just fine. After we
finish the lake country, I'm sure our car will get us
on up to Scotland. I should never have said, 'Oh.'"

"'Nor faithful car to stall...Nor faithful car to
stall.' I'm leaving it just as I wrote it."

"Good."

"I wonder how the kids are?"

"What kids?"

"Our kids, Brandy! There are three: Jimmy, Rosalie and Sue. Remember them?"

"I was kidding, silly. I'm sure Mother has them under control."

"Yeah?"

"Prominent doctors shouldn't say, 'yeah.' They say, yes."

"Yeah?"

"It's okay here with me, but not out in public."

"Well, Brandy, I'll bet that Abe Lincoln himself, as a lawyer and even as President, said 'yeah' anytime he wanted to."

Rog rattled the ice cubes in his glass. Brandy, sitting at a window in the small inn by a beautiful lake, knew that was the signal for a cube or two and another splash of gin. She got up, took his glass and, at the dresser, opened the bottle and poured some gin and dropped more ice into his glass from the bucket.

"Thank you, my dear," Rog said as he took his glass. "None for you?"

"I'll have some wine at dinner as we sit by a picture window overlooking this calm, glass-like lake. It is so lovely."

"The boat ride was fun out there this afternoon. We have been blessed by sunny, warm days since we arrived at Heathrow. We are very lucky. It could be pouring rain this time of year."

"I was so happy, Rog, standing at the rail with you as the boat glided over that clear water. It was divine."

"A bit cool on the water but, yes, it was a wonderful day, all of it, so far. I'm sure there will be some fabulous fresh fish on the menu tonight. I can hardly wait!"

"You know, I'm not the least bit hungry. I feel that we just had lunch."

"We did, Brandy, about four hours ago. It's now almost six. We should probably get downstairs in an hour or so to get a good table by one of those picture windows."

"I may not go, Rog. I may stay right here, with this view of the lake from our room. You can go and have a fine fish dinner. It will be good for you. I think I'll stay in the room. Do you mind?"

Instantly, Rog knew that Brandy's mood had changed slightly and that she was on a mild swing downward. As a doctor, he knew almost all there was to know about a patient with a bipolar illness. He knew that Brandy often couldn't help herself and wouldn't take her medication in more recent months. In fact, recent years. Even Rog's medical skills and long understanding of Brandy's type of problem were to no avail in persuading her to observe a regimen that would keep her on a level plane. To fail her, to be unable to cope with her symptoms as her condition continued to slowly deteriorate, was extremely difficult for Rog.

"Rog?"

"Yes, Brandy."

"I've changed my mind. I would like to join you for dinner downstairs. Do you mind?"

"My dear, I'm delighted."

Roger got up, closed his small notebook and put it on a night-stand along with his glass, and walked to the window where Brandy stood. She turned to him and they embraced.

"I'm so glad we'll go to dinner together, Brandy. You're my love and I want to have you at my side...us...together."

He gently kissed her lips and held her tight for in those few minutes, Roger knew she would be just fine on the rest of their trip. On her own, she had turned away from entering a dark phase of life for her and had bravely challenged herself to meet the light. Perhaps only she knew the powerful tug at her emotions that was required to be more in control of her actions, many of them involuntary. To her, perhaps, it was a temporary, but sweet victory. To Roger, it was much more: she had taken a new, strong stand to fight an infirmity and he was convinced that the will was there for her to regain stability. It was one of Rog's happiest moments.

They showered and changed from their daytime outfits for the boatride and walks that morning. Brandy donned a conservative cocktail/dinner dress, her pearls and her short trimmed hair, streaked with gray to go with her under fifty age, was carefully brushed and glistened in the decreasing sunlight now over the lake.

Rog wore a blazer with brass buttons and gray slacks and his gray hair, worn rather short as perhaps a doctor would, looked youthful for his nearly fifty years.

Rog picked up the room key from the dresser and ushered his "bride" down the hallway and staircase to the lobby and thence into the dining room, where they were seated at the last table for two by a picture window. The sun was a red ball of fire, its bottom edge just on the verge of touching down on the furthest side of the lake. He took Brandy's hands in his.

"That is absolutely gorgeous, Brandy, and I can see the glow of it in your eyes. At first, I wasn't sure that the sun had cast a beautiful light on your eyes or the other way around!"

"You are such a flatterer. I love it."

As they gazed, a waitress appeared at their table.

"Good evening, Dr. and Mrs. Thomas," she said. At the small inn, the employees all used the names of the guests to make the surroundings even more intimate and friendly. This particular inn catered to American tourists and was in a favorite location for travelers en route to Scotland or points south, as well.

"Good evening, young lady," Roger said as Brandy smiled at the pert, red-cheeked girl. "And what is your name?"

"Maria, Sir, thank you."

"I discern a Scandinavian accent, Maria," Rog said.

"Swedish, Sir."

"Ah! You and I may be cousins! My Mother was born in Sweden," Rog continued.

"Would you folks like a beverage before you order?"

"White wine, your house Zinfandel, please. Would that be all right, Brandy?"

"My favorite," Brandy said. "Roger, you always remember."

"Duty of a good husband, my love. Oh, look! The sun has just dipped to the final seconds before setting. A grand view."

"Glorious," said Brandy.

They settled on baked bass, a freshwater perch from the very lake that charmed them. Roasted potatoes and broccoli complemented the fish. Also, fresh spinach salads with a blue cheese dressing for Rog and, for Brandy, a light Honey-Dijon. She was trying to keep her weight under control and often reminded Roger that he should watch his fat intake. She didn't know that he was very meticulously counting the grams and was far below the average recommended. He would have liked more of his patients at the clinic, a part of Johns Hopkins University Hospital, to follow a regimen closer to his own to help regulate the cholesterol count, for one thing. Roger's remained under 200, always. He tried to encourage his patients to be fully aware of an overindulging diet that would lead to complications, especially among the elderly he treated.

"Isn't the countryside of Scotland grand?" Brandy asked. The irregular hills, both high and low, some brownish and some green, the motorways steeper on curving pavement, and the air fresher, were all a delight. Breezes swayed the tall grasses. The ghostly ruins of stone castles, some just a wall or two, of long ago, were seen now and again against gray skies, many as guardians on steep bluffs, watching and waiting to detect any movement below that may foreshadow an advancing army and to ready its hardy defenders for an imminent attack from an ancient foe. One could imagine a multitude of scenarios that were both successful and futile over centuries of bitter rivalries among peoples. Brandy read aloud from some of their guide books once in a while, but was filled with her own thoughts of history learned in schools, as well as imagined, as she viewed the passing landscapes, ever changing, no two scenes alike.

Roger, still somewhat tense at the right hand drive of the English Ford, his left hand rested on the horizonal automatic gear shift for lack of a better use of it. In his Baltimore automobile, his left arm would be on the door rest as his right hand did most of the work. Overseas in Mother England, it was just plain backwards, though he still used his right hand most. And the blasted need to pull off to the left to get petrol or tea nearly infuriated him, so used he was of the right. But, he was on the way, he thought, to mastering the bloody machine.

"Brandy?"

"Yes, dear."

"Would you believe that as I've driven along this rather winding, but well-made road, I've been thinking in some of the stock wording the Brits use."

"Like?"

"Like: 'bloody' as an adjective; 'petrol;' and 'blasted,' too. It is weird as I mentally fret about this bloody car...see, there I go, aloud that time. I do say the people over here do have a very descriptive way with words. They usually leave no doubts in your mind of what they're talking about. Do you have a similar feeling?"

"Well, I have been thinking, as you drive, about those old castles, long vacant, we've seen, about soldiers and bows and arrows, ancient wars among neighboring peoples, moats and drawbridges, clashes of metal weapons, as swords or knives, fire, and the terror the women and children must have suffered within the walls, sturdy then, as their men fought the foe. You get a whole history lesson just driving these roads. But, no, words as you've used, like 'bloody' and 'blasted' and 'petrol' haven't been in my make-believe stories of late. You do understand, do you not, old bean bag?"

"Old bean bag! Marvelous! Brandy, the sharpness of your mind continues to amaze me. You are a card! You waste no blasted words to trick me! I love it!"

"I rather thought, old chap, that, too!" And she laughed.

Rog and Brandy agreed to head for Edinburgh rather than Glasgow because they planned to drive down the east coast all the way to Dover. Glasgow would be, as they read their maps, somewhat out of their way and time was marching on.

They hadn't talked about the quest, mixed in with their vacation and Roger's presentation to the medical conference in London, since they put Bed and Breakfasts on their mental list. Each, independently, had mulled that topic. They both felt it merited serious consideration.

Edinburgh, on the Firth of Forth Inlet, offered grand scenes, especially from its castle dating back to the 11th century. Along Princes Street, after touring the castle, Brandy insisted that Rog buy a Harris Tweed jacket. They were handwoven in the Outer Hebrides, a chain of islands west of Northern Scotland, from Scottish grown wool. There is even a Harris Island about midway in the chain. So, at Dunn & Co., Rog tried on several of the heavy tweeds and, together, he and Brandy decided on a brown one. It had a hat, or cap, to match, but Rog was more hesitant to buy it, let alone try it on. It had a bill on both front and back and, to Rog, looked like the hat worn by the great fictional, London detective, Sherlock Holmes. Brandy thought it was a fine hat, so Rog got it with a strong suspicion in his mind that he'd never wear the bloomin' thing.

Further along the favorite shopping street, Brandy settled on a pleated tartan skirt and decided to get a plaid throw, too, to snuggle up in on cool nights back in Baltimore as she watched television. It would also be a good lap blanket at Oriole baseball games.

Rog wore the new Harris Tweed when they left the men's store, but refused to wear the two-billed hat on the street. He carried it in a shopping bag with his corduroy jacket.

"Rog, the hat would look very good," said Brandy.

"Yeah?"

"Yes."

"But I'd feel like the master detective himself."

"It may not be such a bad idea when we consider that we are looking for a few rare items for the quest."

"If I did, people along the street would wonder where that guy's magnifying glass would be if not in his hand!"

"Don't be ridiculous, Rog."

"Righto, I won't. I won't wear that hat. I can sleuth without both hat and glass. Which reminds me, we best get on with it and stumble into something for our list of one. One won't cut it; we need four, at the very least."

"You know, Rog, the very hat you have in that bag you're carrying could be a market item at home. It might become very faddish."

"Yeah?...I mean, yes?"

"Yes." Brandy thought the hat had class when Rog tried it on in the store. Maybe when they got home and winter weather really set in, Rog might just wear it with his new Harris Tweed. She wouldn't say anything to him, one way or the other. She'd just let him make up his own mind about it. If he got a few compliments on it, perhaps he'd think it looked

okay after all. Oh, Rog had a lot of hats: knit, a
regular cap or two, those kind of caps that are better
in summer than winter, like his Orioles' cap he wore
to games, a fur hat he brought back from a trip to
Russia but never wore, a ski mask, though he never
skied, a homburg he hadn't worn since he and
Brandy went to an inauguration ball years back,
and, of course, had long ago gone out of style as had
men's snap brim felt hats, and he had one or two of
those in the attic somewhere, a straw hat, soft
brimmed, a really fine Icelandic knit cap that was
much better than a Redskin knit hat with a gold
tassel on top. Well, she thought, enough on hats. She
had one last thought, however, that, if she threw all
of them out, the only one he'd ever ask for to wear
would be the Oriole cap he wore when Cal Ripken,
Jr. eclipsed the old Lou Gehrig record for consecutive
games played. That was a proud night for that cap
of his for Rog was under it.

They started their drive down the east coast
and, with no interest in golf, Rog wasn't inclined to
stop at the St. Andrews course where the game
originated, and they did stay over at Berwick-upon-
Tweed.

In the dining room of what Brandy described as
a quaint and divine small inn, Brandy opened her
small hand bag and removed a piece of paper.

"I have something to read to you, Rog. Do you
mind?"

"Of course not. Please."

"You won't be upset or laugh, will you?"

"Not unless it's a hilarious joke. Go ahead."

"Very well, then...
'We drove on up to Scotland,
And marveled at the sight,
Of rolling hills all capped in green,
To match the tartan bright.

'There, dined in regal splendor,
In room where grace abounds,
Took our coffee in the parlor,
Midst gentlemen with hounds.'"
"Is that it?" Rog asked.
"It is."
"Brandy, it is marvelous! When in the world did you write it?"
"The words came to me while you were in the shower."
"I love it! First class! Would you consider incorporating it into mine?"
"You know I would."
"It is really good! You have hidden talents I didn't dream you had! Here's a man, Brandy, that couldn't be more proud of his wife. Say, old girl, how about us taking turns with a couple of verses as we go along?"
"I'd like that."
"Not to change the subject, but have you given any thought as to what we bring home to the kids?"
"I've thought of it off and on. Just that last shopping with Rosalie, well...it is so difficult to buy clothes they'd wear."
"You keep an eye for the girls; I'll concentrate on Jimmy."

It had been a week, at least, when the drive in
the rented Ford, all 2000 miles of it, came to an end
in Dover. Their next planned stop was in Brugge,
just across the English Channel in Belgium. It was
a charming city with many canals and they took a
small boat near the hotel with a boatman who was
young and wore local kind of clothes, but set it off
with an oversized tam such as painters of old wore
at their canvas. He spoke good English and narrated
his "tourist tale" as he moved the small boat with a
long pole that set the boat proceeding on a leisurely
pace. And he smiled a lot. He must have been a
happy fellow in his work.

At dinner that evening, Rog read:
"'Boated across the Channel,
To visit just a while,
We loved the lilting language there,
And people with a smile.

'And Brugge was something special,
'Tis Venice of that land,
We glided ancient waterways,
Our boatman, too, was grand!'"
"How nice, Rog! You captured the whole scene in
those few lines," Brandy said, "and I say bravo!"

Back in their room for the night, England now
behind them, Rog told Brandy they had driven about
2000 miles in making the grand loop from London to
Bath, points west in the Lake Country, north to
Scotland and down the east coast to Dover where
they left the car and boated to Belgium.

"Much further than I imagined," Brandy said. "The week or more has flown by and nearly half our quest time is gone, Rog."

"I know."

"But, Rog, I just had an idea at dinner I want to discuss with you. It came to me when our waiter brought those tasty, warm dinner buns before our salads and as we enjoyed our wine."

"Those rolls or buns were great! I was afraid my intake of those dratted fat grams would exceed my limit and ruin my dinner, besides. Did you like the lamb?"

"It was cooked to perfection. Wish I could prepare it that way at home. Anyway, Rog, the fresh, hot buns tonight triggered something I think may be worth giving our deep thought. You do remember Bath?"

"Yes. That was our stop after Hampton Court of Henry VIII."

"Right. And you remember having tea in the Pump Room at those marble Roman baths?"

"I do."

"Did we have scones?"

"Those biscuitlike little cakes?"

"Right," confirmed Brandy.

"Well...I don't think we did for some reason or other."

"We did not. But, did we see in a display counter there other sweet rolls, etc.?"

"I think that counter was right by the cash register. Where is this going, Brandy?"

"Just a sec: in that case by the cash register did you happen to notice big buns, like hamburger buns, but twice as big?"

"Frankly, no. I don't remember big buns...in the case."

"Rog! Well, those big guys are called Bath Buns."

"So, at the famous Knott's Berry Farm in California they sell jams and jellies. What is so different about selling Bath Buns in Bath?"

"Roger, why not introduce those Bath Buns into the U.S. of A.?"

"Maybe they are."

"No. They are not sent to the United States. I asked the lady at the cash register while you got the change from our check and walked outside to take some pictures and look at that huge marble swimming pool built by the Romans."

"How can you remember all that?"

"Maybe I thought it was important. Anyway, Rog, how does this strike you? We put Bath Buns on our list for 'Win' and, Roger, dear, since America took the Thomas' English Muffins and brought them there, why wouldn't it make economic sense for some of 'Win''s associates to market Bath Buns there?"

"Do these Bath Buns have all those little nooks and crannies and the holes inside them to catch the butter? Thomas' English Muffins are a very big item in our country."

"Probably they do and I also imagine sales of those Thomas' English Muffins are in the millions of dollars. I picked up this little sheet about the history of Bath Buns and put it in my purse. I'll study it tonight in our room and give you a quick, succinct report. How's that?"

"Fine! You may have something!"

Back in their room, Roger read a local newspaper, closed his eyes for a while and then turned on the television to watch and listen to the local language. Brandy sat at a small writing desk at one wall and made some notes. Roger finally turned off the television and got into his pajamas.

"Are you ready, Roger?"

"For...what?"

"Roger, you're so naughty at times!"

"Let me hear your report."

"In 1680, a French Huguenot girl refugee from France, named Sally Lunn, found employment with a baker, who had premises in Lilliput Alley very close to the Abbey Church in the Spa City of Bath. She introduced the baker to the French brioche type breads, or buns, that were later on to become famous and forever associated with her name, the original bakery building and indeed the City of Bath."

"What does brioche bread mean?" Rog asked.

"A soft, light-textured roll or bun made from eggs, butter, flour and yeast in a secret recipe."

"It may be a bit tough on cholesterol, but I think it's a winner!"

"Oh, Rog..."

"Put it on our list as number 1! And then, Mrs. Thomas, come to bed!"

EIGHT

Clay would have given a lot just to know of the trials and tribulations that Travis and Roger went through during the days that had elapsed to that point into the quest. For his part, he felt as taut as the mainspring of a newly-wound mantel clock. He had to relax. The meetings, oral presentations to the Asian mission chiefs and his full and hectic schedule, including social functions and planned trips, to say nothing of the long air flights and staff cars that took him to the right place at the right time, wore on him.

In the Singapore airport, he put pen to paper and wrote, without undo flair, of his present state of mind as he sat nearly half way around the world. Clay wrote:

"This quest...this game...is gnawing at my gut day and night...never ceasing...wracking my body, my mind with a constant pain...crowding other more important thoughts I must have and duties I must perform for State...taking a toll on me physically and mentally that I can not measure with any surety. It stretches the very limits a man can endure. It has become vile, a sickness, a cancer that can't be cured because it's everywhere inside me, every fiber, nerve and muscle, and all around me, wherever I go, whatever I do, whenever I think of it or imagine it, even faintly, it becomes magnified and somehow overbearing until I feel helpless, devoid of normal strengths of feelings and physical actions to the point of wanting to end it all, not soon...but, now...right now. A man can't do two things at once...his job and this obsession of seeking, ever seeking and thinking of something that is really extraneous to my very being, yet having an exaggerated effect on me...even within...a total effect. Two weeks ago, at the beginning, I knew I could handle it and was eager to get on with it...and last week it got tougher and now...now it is insufferable, debilitating, it has me off balance, wavering, groping like a blind person newly afflicted with a wretched handicap, wanting to beat it, beat the rap, defeat it with some inner strength I couldn't even know for certain was there...but now, it is almost too late...to go on or to quit...it's a trap. But, I'm on a mission, a special mission, I must see through. I'm at the point of no return, both my job and this other thing...I must go on and finish both of them..."

Clay stopped writing. He put the cap on his pen, clipped it onto his inside breast pocket and then...he ripped up the sheets of paper and put them into a receptacle by his chair in the waiting area.

Looking back, after that brief stopover in Singapore and the continuing flight to Indonesia, he seemed to get a second wind. He could scarcely remember what he had written earlier in the Singapore airport as he waited for his plane and now for the embassy car in Jakarta to come to his hotel for him. He felt refreshed and ready, amazingly, for the Jakarta part of the trip to commence. He may have had a premonition that Jakarta would yield a badly needed gift for him: to see his meetings through in a good manner and, perhaps, then he would discover something very important to grow his short quest list to a few more choices than that with which he had arrived.

It was a spooky flight from Singapore. There was heavy rain and lightning as the plane taxied for take off. Never did really get out of rough air all the way to Jakarta. However, there were enough breaks in the clouds below to see, once again, as he had on various of his previous flights, beauteous islands, so calm and lush and elegant, with surrounding blue-green waters and many tantalizing beaches of white sand that seemed to beg for Clay's footprints. The green-patched fields and red-tiled clustered houses were impressive to see and a reminder of those many graceful, Spanish-style California homesites, to name a few, as in Sacramento, San Francisco, Santa Barbara and San Diego, with their trademark red-tile roofing.

Upon landing at Jakarta, Clay's escort officer from the embassy walked him through customs and delivered him to a grand hotel, The Ambassador, where he then awaited transportation to the Ambassador's residence for a wedding reception for the Personnel Director and his bride.

In the lobby, seated at a good vantage point to see cars that passed by the front of the hotel, Clay watched them for a time, looked at his watch, and was sure he had the time right for when the embassy car was due. It was difficult to know the makes of many of the automobiles he saw, especially the foreign made and, now, it seemed hard to even recognize American models.

Suddenly, Clay took a small notebook from his pocket, the inside breast one, opened it to a clean sheet, uncapped his pen and began to write, furiously, the following:

"Many years ago, I had a brother-in-law who was an auto mechanic. His name doesn't even come to me readily, but that is of no import. In World War II, he was a master sergeant with the 8th Air Force in England, and headed a maintenance unit, at a certain American air field, where they were charged with keeping the B-17's and B-24's flying over Western Europe. When the war ended, he returned to his adopted state of Montana and set up a small auto shop as the sole mechanic and his reputation quickly spread throughout the community. He was the best mechanic they ever had, honest and was able to service enough cars to make a good living wage in that part of the country. Well, this background on the ex-brother-in-law, while really unnecessary then, leads to something he predicted in all seriousness in the late 1940's: someday, cars would have a single bar, like a fluorescent light tube, to replace the usual dual headlights now on automobiles. It would be perfected, he said, by automobile manufacturing engineers and would revolutionize automobile headlights as we have known them over the years. The new headlights would project a solid beam of a powerful light, like a sheet of light, if you will, that would give drivers more reliable road light at night. Mark my words, he said. The single tube of light would come one day, just as surely as radio and air-conditioning, and would become standard equipment on automobiles before the end of this century and millennium."

Clay reread the notes he just completed. Great Caesar! he thought. Could that automobile innovation, predicted nearly half a century ago, be an item to add to the list? Clay was excited to the point of getting up from the sofa where he had waited and he paced about the huge lobby in a great circle. But, he wondered, could this new auto light best be categorized as an object or as a remembrance of a person? An object; a remembrance? As he circled, he suddenly noted a man in step with him near the registration desk.

"Mr. Stevenson?" said the man.

Clay looked at him for an instant and continued to pace, then stopped abruptly.

"You, sir, are you from the American embassy?"

"That I am. I'm your driver to take you to the reception at the residence."

"Of course! Forgive me! I had something on my mind that seemed to require me to pace up and down as I waited. Sorry you had to come in. I should have been ready to spot you out front and join you there."

"Think nothing of it, Mr. Stevenson. Are you ready?"

"Quite. Thank you."

They went from the lobby to the car out front and Clay relaxed in the back seat on the ride to the residence.

Once there, he mingled and was introduced to many of the American and Indonesian guests. It was most festive; he had a photo taken with the Ambassador's wife and, then, other dignitaries. After a polite, but brief, stay, the escort officer and he went to downtown Jakarta and, from the 28th floor of a new Japanese hotel, joined four couples for a Chinese dinner, which was on a par, or maybe superior, to any he had enjoyed in Hong Kong. They had a large ringside table for a continuous floor show: vocalists, a German acrobat and his Herculean, blond female partner, and good music. After the usual number of too many Chinese courses, they went to the escort officer's home for brandy and conversation. Clay gave them a brief rundown on the Hong Kong conference and organizational changes for some embassies around the world. Clay was flattered when one of the wives told him he looked like Billy Graham!

Next morning, Clay and two men from the embassy went to the mountains. It was a Sunday and to American employees there, the mountain trip away from Jakarta was like going to the beach from Washington, D.C. to escape the oppressive humidity in summer.

In one small part of Indonesia, Clay saw on the ground what he had not seen from the air: the small villages and fields and hills and, perhaps most importantly, the people scattered through some amazing countryside. People and traffic, like on a holiday, made their way to the coolness of the mountains, one nearly 9,000 feet high. Even with air-conditioning in the car, Clay's shirt stuck to his back even before the slow climb up the mountainous roads began. The difference in temperature as they got higher was pleasant indeed. Countless vendors, fruit stands and small organized communities along the highway, a narrow two-laner, were seen. They saw beautiful, colorful indigenous costumes; all modes of transportation – from foot to horse to bicycles to three-wheeled cars to pedi-taxis to Mercedes. And there were exotic fruits to buy along the route. One, called durian, and that looked like a green-skinned coconut with spikes, was supposed to cause a craving for it, once tasted.

When Clay later learned that the durian or durion, a Malay thorn, the large oval or globose fruit of a tree of the East Indian Islands, had a hard prickly rind, a soft cream-colored pulp, a most delicious flavor, but an offensive odor, with seeds that were roasted and eaten like chestnuts, he decided he wouldn't add it to his list for "Win." And, so, Clay didn't take the first taste, either.

The car finally arrived at Puncak Mountain Pass, but, while en route, Clay saw a palace and a city called Bogor, with some one million people.

The destination, the home that two of the embassy staff owned, had beautiful grounds and gardens and a great panoramic view of many surrounding green foothills and mountains. Mammoth tea groves on hillsides were everywhere.

The coolness, a lot of rain and conversation, cheese and cold cuts and beer, and those wonderful vistas, made for an interesting and pleasant interlude. They also visited a nearby market and botanical gardens. But Clay was soon tired by the heavy rain during the return to Jakarta and the blinding car lights that faced them in traffic all the way down the mountain and they slowly felt the heat rise as they descended.

Next morning, Clay breakfasted in the hotel's Arafura Room before a planned visit to a school, a warehouse, a luncheon, a visit to Mini-Indonesia, like Disneyland, and a fancy dinner at the home of the Deputy Chief of Mission.

Clay knew that the Republic of Indonesia was formerly the Netherlands East Indies or the Dutch East Indies, but he found it extremely difficult to keep track of the maze of islands, large and small, that made up the old Dutch empire. Jakarta, the capital, was on the Isle of Java, while other islands included Sumatra, Sulawesi, Moluccas, Timor, West Irian on New Guinea and Kalimantan on Borneo, and Bali, a tiny island off the eastern tip of Java, and many lesser islands, all constituted present-day Indonesia. It was part of Clay's business to get to know it well.

The American school he visited was ultra-modern and completely equipped. Clay told the superintendent from Washington state that they didn't have schools like that when he was growing up. The school, campus-style and functional, was impressive by any standards and especially in the Western Pacific.

The stop at the Mini-Indonesia Complex was exceptionally informative about the regions that made up Indonesia. The exhibitions included typical buildings and Clay ascended a notched-log ladder to see a display of artifacts inside a large wooden hut on stilts. An indigenous man inside, alone in the structure, startled Clay when first he saw him and even more so when the man took a blowgun from a wall and demonstrated the native art of the use of poisonous darts against prey and, perhaps, even their enemies. Clay later shook hands with him, as a friend would. After seeing an impressive array of knives and spears, Clay backed down the crude ladder, very carefully, in a sweat.

On the Mini-Indonesia grounds, Clay happened to walk across a patch of grass near a sidewalk and his escort asked him to look where he had walked. It was full of a lawn-level fern that, when touched with the toe of your shoe, closed like a trap! The fern stayed in that position about five minutes and then opened up again. Clay imagined he might be eaten alive before he reached the sidewalk. How exotic can plants get?

At breakfast in his hotel the next morning, the jam for Clay's toast was not some delectable, wondrous flavor from a fruit on a hidden island in the region...it was strawberry from a slick package by Kraft!

He spent a long day at the embassy, toured every office and shook a lot of hands. It was like a political campaign. Overseas department employees were always glad to see a visiting officer from Washington with the hope that some outstanding points on personnel could be reported on his return to Main State. Four staffers asked for information on overtime, leave, the normal questions from those in the field.

Clay was shown a new advancement in communications at the embassy. Secret embassy "bugging" by other nations had been a worldwide practice and problem since mini-scaled electronic devices were developed decades ago. Some, rather most, embassies, foreign and domestic, had sought to preclude the leakage of their most sensitive messages, verbal and cable, to a potential enemy in both the political and economic areas. Our government had developed "plastic cocoons" large enough in which to hold high level discussions of top secret information with a surety that more conventional eavesdropping equipment couldn't penetrate. The chances were good that, since the innovation of the cocoon rooms, advanced technology had found ways to penetrate even those state-of-the-art meeting places. To be inside a cocoon was not unlike being in a glassed-over hot house, but with certain expectation that it was impenetrable.

To Clay, invited into such a cocoon, it was devoid of fresh air and created something of a ring by air pressure in his ears, as often happens in aircraft flights, and one seems to need to clear their sensitive eardrums back to normal. Perhaps a longer stay, than just minutes, does not present this problem. But even for a short visit, the plastic cocoon made one feel like sitting inside a cramped telephone booth.

It wasn't until the next morning that Clay focused on the cocoon as perhaps having some commercial value and may well warrant a place on his short list for "Win." Chances, however, were that, if all cocoons in use around the world floated up into space to engulf the planet, an astronaut's view of the phenomenon would not be unlike two scoops of vanilla ice cream put into a glass, topped with root beer and, then, better look out for bubbles that career up and over the edge of the glass, irrepressibly, as the treat-maker gives the concoction a vigorous stir with a long spoon.

A staff car took Clay to the airport and he'd be on his way to Singapore for a four-hour layover before continuing on to Bangkok. There was a twelve-hour difference in time between Jakarta and Washington, D.C. As Clay had a 6 A.M. cup of coffee, some of his colleagues at Main State were about to have cocktails before dinner.

On the plane, Clay thought of two gifts, perhaps, that had presented themselves to him while in Jakarta: the tube auto light and the cocoon. The automobile light seemed the more practical one to consider for the list. Not many folks were without automobiles in the United States and so the demand for them, should they come into being, would have a huge market in the nation, not to say other more developed countries in the world. On the other hand, the cocoon merits, while few, certainly eclipsed the exotic fruit, though with a delicious flavor, the offensive odor may be impossible to eliminate even by talented fruit processors. To Clay's mind, the fruit was out.

NINE

"Just remember, Ainsley, that there are probably more minor earthquakes in Southern California in a month than there are in Costa Rica in a year," Travis told her to lend some comfort.

"But I don't like that weird feeling when the floor moves and you have a sense of helplessness."

"Did you see that Canadian nurse, who stood near us in the park before we were allowed to go back into the hotel?"

"Guess not."

"I couldn't tell whether she had a robe on or if she was in her nightie."

"Did it matter?"

"Well..."

"And how did you know she was a Canadian nurse, Travis?"

"Well... yes, I recall I spoke to her in the lobby when I went down to get a newspaper the other morning. You were doing your hair."

"I see."

"Well, you were!"

"What color was it?"

"What?"

"Her 'nightie?'"

"Damned if I know."

"Travis, I don't see how you walked so fast with those stitches to get out of the hotel when it swayed." She changed the subject.

"You know, I don't either. Better the painful pulls at my stomach than a ceiling on my whole body!"

"I would think so!"

"You know, I think that Costa Rican doctor did exploratory surgery on me. I don't think he knew if I had appendicitis or not. You did see the incision...it was vertical and, what, about five inches long?"

"I guess. Did the Canadian nurse know?"

"She guessed exploratory, too."

"Travis! Did you show her your incision?"

"Of course not! When she saw me walking slowly in the lobby, I told her I just had an emergency appendectomy, and described the incision. You know how patients like to tell about their operations. Well, she said it should have been smaller and on the lower right."

"I'd just as soon not hear more before break-fast...if I can eat."

"Ainsley..."

"Get dressed, so we can go to the dining room."

Over breakfast, Ainsley said she'd like to go to Nicaragua.

"Fine! To Managua?"

"Might as well. Are you up to traveling?... Guess you are."

"Stitches out this morning so we'll be free to go, sure!"

"And ask your 'Ben Casey' what he did to get your appendix out...exploratory or regular."

"That I will. Want me to call the airline office for tickets?"

"When you're at the doctor's office, I'll call from here at the hotel."

"A morning flight would probably be best, or afternoon, so we can see the countryside down there. I wouldn't want to fly at night."

"Nor I."

Later that morning, Travis arrived at their hotel by cab. The stitches were gone and, of course, Travis forgot to ask about the scar. He figured it really didn't make a damn, either way. He had survived and that was a good sign all was well.

Over lunch at a restaurant a block or so from their hotel, Ainsley and Travis discussed the after-noon flight, really a short hop from San Jose to

Managua. They'd probably fly over the large Lake of Nicaragua.

"We should shop for a souvenir or two for home and your office," Ainsley suggested.

"Probably a good store between here and the hotel and then we could pack."

"Right on, Counselor," Ainsley answered. Her peeve seemed to be over.

Their flight got off the ground a bit late so that an engine on the starboard side could be checked after it coughed and quit as the old craft taxied to the runway. Declared okay by a small ground crew, that included a baggage handler or two, they had lifted off safely.

Some twenty minutes into the flight, the right motor coughed and quit, the propeller twisting to a complete stop. Travis and Ainsley were on the right side of the plane and saw the engine when it puffed out white smoke and quit.

"Travis!"

"Now, Ainsley, these local airlines are not like those at home."

"We should have rented a car!"

"Try to relax."

Suddenly, one of the two men in the plane's nose, the co-pilot, no doubt, burst out the doorway into the cabin and spoke in rapid Spanish.

"What's he saying?" asked Ainsley.

"I don't know. Let me listen," Travis answered. He had taken Spanish in college, but the co-pilot had tossed in a local dialect that made it difficult to know all the words that spewed out.

"Travis, we're going down!"

"Easy, sweetheart."

"We're going down!"

"Señor, por favor. ¿Qué pasa?" Travis yelled over the other motor's noise as it began to sputter, too.

"Emergency! Emergency!" came English words from the co-pilot's lips. Travis tried to make out the new words in Spanish he then spoke.

"We're off course to the east and we're going to crash-land!" Travis heard enough to translate those words for Ainsley. "Hold on!

"Buckle that seat belt, Ains! Hurry!"

There were screams and cries from other panicked passengers, mostly Latinos. The co-pilot ran forward and slammed the cabin door.

"Travis! Travis! We're about to head over water! And we're almost to the ground!"

"The crew kept the plane level. We'll pancake down! Hold on, Ains! Hold on!"

The screams from passengers and the sound of grinding metal of the plane's belly on the trees and ground seemed unending, but the plane had cut through thick jungle that slowed it and then Travis saw the beach and the surf as the plane ground to a stop.

"Travis! We're in water!"

"Barely! Unbuckle and come on," he shouted to her as he headed for the opening in the side of the plane where there was once a door.

"Travis! Wait for me! Travis!"

Travis turned and grabbed her and they jumped together out the hole in the plane and splashed into the water. Some passengers slammed into the water almost on top of them.

"Swim, Ains! Swim like hell!"

"Travis!"

"Swim!" Travis locked one arm around her head, now finally up and out of the water and, in minutes, he was dragging Ainsley up onto the beach. He pulled her by her arms as far as he could and reached dry sand. He fell, exhausted, at her side. He remembered seeing two or three people in the water behind him, but now they were gone from sight. He saw the smashed remains of the plane bob up and down in the surf, for much of it was still in the tangle of jungle growth at the land edge of the beach. He rolled Ainsley onto her back and began mouth-to-mouth resuscitation. He pressed on her chest. Then, mouth-to-mouth. Again, then, again.

Suddenly she choked, he rolled her to her side and she gasped for air as seawater and sand spewed from her mouth.

"Ains! Ains!" Travis yelled.

She gagged and more water, sand and her lunch flowed out. But, in moments, she was getting air, slowly, but getting air back into her lungs and horrid gobs of vile vomit out.

"Trav...!"

"Don't talk! Breathe! Damn it! Breathe!"

She turned to her back and he used his shirt sleeve to wipe away the sand and food from her mouth and nose. In moments, she took her first deep breath and turned again on her side. Her skirt was gone and blouse half ripped off. But she was still and breathed steadily and audibly as her chest heaved.

"Thank God! Thank God! Ains! Thank God!"

"Travis..."

"Don't talk!"

Travis ripped off his torn and bloody shirt. He tossed it over her bare chest.

"Trav...okay?"

"Okay, sweetheart, okay."

Travis looked at her eyes as she opened and closed them. They were red. Probably sand. He listened as he knelt by her side. He heard the surf pound onto the beach on rolling, large waves. He saw a part of the plane in the water still tossing to and fro. He didn't hear a human voice. Maybe some were too far away to hear them. Maybe at the edge of the jungle, maybe in the bobbing wreckage of the plane, maybe out in the surf. He and Ainsley were alive. Maybe the only ones. There were ten or twelve on the plane as it left San Jose...and the two up front in the pilot's cockpit. He tried to stand up but sank back to his knees. He stood again. He looked up and down the beach as the light of the sun was cut by white, fluffy clouds and then it was bright again. Neither up nor down the beach did he see anything. He looked at a crushed gash in the jungle that had pushed toward the beach and was long halted in its growth. It was doubtless the spot where some of the plane slid through the tangle to the water.

And then he was aware of excited voices that seemed to get louder and louder. The sounds came from the jungle side, not the beach. For not a thing moved, save him and Ainsley's heaving chest, now more regular and less labored. Thank God! Thank God! he thought and then he heard his own words that nearly screamed in his ears. He fell to the sand and passed out. Ainsley reached and found his hand and held it tight as she coughed up more vomit but, thank the good Lord, she was breathing and Travis soon stirred to consciousness as her hand still gripped his. Now she heard voices nearby and a number of people rushed to them on the beach. They had blankets and used them to carry Ainsley first and then Travis from the hot sand and into the cool of the jungle, talking all the while, loudly, in Spanish to a point near hysteria.

As Ainsley and Travis lurched back and forth, to and fro in the blankets, as their rescuers carried them inland, they seemed to lose all sense of direction other than the sounds of the pounding surf that seemed to dim as they rolled back and forth and tree limbs and leaves, giant green ones, slapped at or near their faces and the full length of their bodies. Once, Travis rolled off the blanket onto the ground and felt many hands pick him up and into the blanket again and the swaying began anew as the gait of the bearers increased. It must have been that a clearing was reached, for tree limbs and leaves and the rustle of brush near them stopped. Travis could feel that his hands and arms had been cut and Ainsley, he thought, may be in pain from cuts, too.

"Travis! Travis!"

"Ainsley! I'm right here."

"Where?"

"I'm in a room next to yours."

"Thank God! I woke up and I was alone. I'm on a cot."

"Me, too. And I'm bandaged."

"You are? Where?"

"My right shoulder and left arm. Stings a little. Are you in bandages?"

"My ribs. They hurt. I can see a scrape on my left arm, but no bandage. Maybe some iodine or...what's that other stuff? I remember it as a kid."

"Merc..."

"That's it. Mercurochrome."

"On the scrape?"

"Swathed all over it, yes."

"And the ribs?"

"I just now see tape all around my rib cage clear up to my boobs. It's so damn tight! At least I have a sheet over me and I just lifted it up to see the tape a sec ago."

"I slept. You must have, too."

"I still feel the grit of sand in my mouth. Gag!"

"Wonder where we are?"

"We are at a clinic in Bluefields. I saw a sign as we came in."

"Where in hell is that?"

"On the Caribbean coast of Nicaragua directly across from Managua on the Pacific."

"Missed our destination, eh?"

"Travis, don't make me laugh; it hurts!"

"Sorry. Who told you that?"

"A lady who taped me up spoke a bit of English. It took her a while and me a while to figure it out."

"We better try to get word to the U.S. Embassy in Managua and have them get us out of here."

"You try your Spanish on whoever comes in next. Okay?"

"Right. Or a phone."

Just then, a uniformed officer, a gun on his hip and in fatigues, boots and all, came into the doorless room where Travis was on a cot. A local joined the officer at the doorway.

"Señor, por favor, un momento..." Travis said.

"You are an American?" said the officer in perfect English.

"Yes, indeed."

"Do you have your passport?"

"It may be in my pants or..."

"There is nothing in this room but you on that cot, my friend."

"We were in a plane crash en route from San Jose..."

"We know all of that. And the woman in the next room?"

"My wife. My name is Travis Goodson and I guess some locals brought us here from the beach."

"So they did."

"Can we call Managua, the American Embassy? They can verify our identities."

"That isn't necessary, Señor."

"But we need to get to Managua. We have hotel reservations waiting..."

"Señor, it will be impossible for you to leave this building, this local clinic. You came, by accident, if you will allow a simple joke...forgive me...and I have my instructions to detain you..."

"How long? We're American citizens..."

"But you nor your wife have passports and are in our country illegally..."

"We can't help that!"

"I will be in touch with Managua and, if certain conditions are met..."

"What conditions?"

"Let us say, $20,000..."

"Are we your prisoners? Hostages? I am not unfamiliar with international law..."

"Save your strength, Señor. We know who you are and, if conditions are met..."

"This is outrageous to hold Americans against our will!"

"Señor, you are in Nicaragua."

"Well, than tell the American Embassy to pay the money and get us to Managua!"

"Good evening, Mr. Goodson."

"What? Are you leaving us? Are you keeping us here? And for how long?"

"Sleep well, Señor."

Travis listened as the army boots strode away and the sound of a local's sandals shuffled on the floor and out of earshot.

"Ainsley!" Travis called.

"Ainsley!" He sat on the edge of his cot, then saw a chain from one of his legs to a bar on his high window.

"Ainsley! Ainsley!"

The two-wheeled cart, filled with straw and grass, pulled by a horse, bumped along on a hole-pitted road of dirt, even the horse stumbling now and then causing the cart to shake and rock. Two men stood at the front of the cart holding the reins and urged the thin horse on by a whip that cracked in the air or across the back of the animal. It would run faster for a time and then slow down under the weight it pulled.

Ainsley, on the straw in the cart, was blindfolded. She was on her back and an old woman sat by her. The ache and steady pain of her ribs in the twisting, turning cart were almost unbearable.

"Travis?" she called. "Travis!" "Travis!"

"Shut that gringo up, old woman!" shouted one of the drivers.

The old woman's large, rough hand was cupped tightly over Ainsley's mouth for a few minutes.

Ainsley fell silent and moved her left leg first, very slowly, and then her right. As her feet touched the sides of the small cart, she knew that Travis had been left behind when she was gagged and carried by blanket to the cart. She was alone with two rough-talking men and an old woman. The gag had been removed but she could see nothing. They might be able to keep her from seeing and yelling, but Ainsley knew they could never stop her from thinking.

She thought longingly of Travis, the trip to Central America, her petty peeve at Travis on the subject of the Canadian nurse in San Jose, how he was so brave and saved her life after the plane crash when he dragged her from the surf and drowning. He had saved her life! What could be more dear than one's life? And she owed him her love and the very life she had coursing through her veins and the very air she breathed. Travis saved all of that.

And, what of him? The ring of her name in her ears as he called out to her when she was taken from the clinic, she still heard those loud calls, wondering why she didn't answer and left wondering what may have happened to her. Would she ever see and hear and be near him again? Thank goodness for her private thoughts of him but even they brought pain to her. Ainsley couldn't tell how much time had elapsed, but it seemed she heard some new sounds and the road the cart had earlier bumped along, now seemed smooth and she could hear the wooden wheels rolling now on asphalt, maybe, or concrete. But it was smooth. And her ribs didn't ache so much, now that the tossing and turns she experienced had ceased.

Suddenly, the cart stopped. She heard the two men jump down from the cart. She felt the old woman remove her blindfold. It hurt her eyes, the brightness, and the smell of oil and gas nearly gagged her. She was finally able to focus her eyes. She was on an airstrip, right by a small plane as dusk approached. She was gently lifted from the cart.

"Where are we? Who are you? Where are you taking me? Where is my husband?" she asked in quick succession.

"Mrs. Goodson, you are in safe hands," said the old woman. "I am a local hire of the American Embassy in Managua. These two men are also employees there of the government of the United States. We have succeeded in rescuing you from the clinic and, now that we are out of rebel-held territory, this small plane from Managua will fly you there and the pilot will turn you over to American authorities from the Embassy."

"Señora," said one of the men, "we regret the rough treatment of you we employed to convince the rebels we were taking you to another rebel stronghold. Forgive us, but you are safe."

"Travis, what about my husband?" she asked as tears welled in her eyes.

"He, too, has been 'captured' by us 'rebels' and awaits you in Managua. He is fine!"

Ainsley sobbed for joy, as she was led over to the plane and helped aboard.

"Thank you, thank you, thank you...," she called as the motor of the plane started and the two men removed their hats and waved them as the old woman dried her own tears with the crude blindfold, smiled and waved to Ainsley as the plane moved

away for take off. They were only a few minutes from
Managua.

Travis, his arm in a sling and a broad smile on
his face as tears streamed down his cheeks, was on
the tarmac as the small plane landed and taxied to
the small buildings for non-commercial aircraft.

Ainsley was carefully taken from the plane,
placed in a wheelchair and Travis ran toward her as
embassy employees wheeled the chair away from the
plane.

"Ainsley! Ainsley! My love," Travis cried as he
reached for her and nearly smothered her in hugs
and kisses.

"Travis, darling! I'm so happy to see you!"

By the time they reached the embassy car awaiting them, they were told that a friend of theirs sent
his highest regards and wished them well as their
Central America trip continued.

"Who was it?" Travis asked as Ainsley anxiously
awaited for the name.

"He is in Bangkok, or was, this friend of yours.
Name of Clay Stevenson. Know him?" asked the
embassy staffer.

The Goodsons were examined at the American
Hospital in Managua, X-rays, new tapings, bandages and a sling for Travis and were pronounced
sound by American doctors. They were personal,
overnight guests of the ambassador at the residence

who arranged a small cocktail party and dinner in their honor.

Next morning, as a precaution, they were supplied with new passports and driven in the ambassador's car to Tegucigalpa, Honduras, put up in a fine hotel, were wished good luck on the remainder of their tour of Central America and good hunting in the quest, now drawing rapidly to an end.

TEN

From the Singapore Airport, Clay taxied directly to the Raffles Hotel, famed landmark and stopover place for many generations of talented people of the arts on the world scene and for discerning tourists from many diverse lands as well. Clay was about to become one of those tourists with four hours at the incomparable Raffles Hotel until flight time to Bangkok.

Though there was a downpour when Clay arrived at the airport, he didn't alter an iota of his prearranged plan for a hasty shopping trip to the Raffles. He wished to ask of a special kind of earrings he had heard about on his recent travels and they were on his mind for Jamie. She had been kind enough to send along a birthday gift for him when he reached Bangkok and he felt inclined to reciprocate. He had learned that the earrings were in a small shop off the lobby of the old hotel. Further, he was determined to see the Long Bar, a watering hole over the years for the likes of Rudyard Kipling, who chose the Raffles for his gin and inspiration. With only four hours between planes, Clay hoped to get the earrings and as much inspiration as time allowed.

The front door of the hotel still had a gallant, uniformed doorman who met every car and welcomed its occupants. As Clay arrived, the smiling doorman was at the door of the taxi with a colorful umbrella held over Clay's head until he was well under the portico.

The first views of the grand lobby and main desk were exhilarating. Mammoth columns, ceiling fans and chandeliers and many people, some who hurried, some who strolled, waiters who served tea to individuals or small groups seated at tables along the lobby's walls, and many high-ceiling corridors leading away from the lobby-level. One such corridor led to the jewelry shop where Clay inquired of the earrings and was shown a variety of them. The very ones he sought were there: they were neither of precious metal nor gem. They were made of cloth, a satiny, shiny delicate kind, perhaps of silk. But their color was everything: a pastel of shimmering pink. They were alive with a beautiful simplicity and an iridescent sheen. Clay knew they would please, bought them and proceeded to the Long Bar, where, rather than the Singapore Gin Sling, Clay settled for a British-style gin and tonic: no ice.

Though it was lunch time, the bar was nearly empty. Clay sat near the iron-grilled open porch where ceiling fans and the breezes were a delight. It was eighty-four degrees in Singapore and cloudy. Three waiters, the bartender and the three English women who had just sat down at the table by him were the only ones in the bar. Not that Clay eavesdropped, but the ladies spoke of Malaysian religion, which was way over his head. He heard only because of their proximity.

Clay turned his attention to his gin and journal and wrote in it that the famous jazzman, Ray Charles, and his orchestra were on the same plane with him from Jakarta to Singapore. Since there was so much action in front of him, Clay was the last to deplane and claim his luggage. He watched patiently as the bass fiddles and drums and all the other instruments found their way to baggage claim by conveyor belt. There was no piano aboard.

With his gin gone, the English ladies gone and his journal closed, Clay moved out into the lobby and took a table opposite the entrance to the Tiffin Dining Room and ordered tea and watched the people go to and fro. One was a young and beautiful Chinese girl, he guessed. She was dressed to kill, but Clay hoped not. A British Colonel with a swagger stick and proud as a peacock passed by. Then, the Chinese girl again. She had a body not unlike a Tab girl in a television commercial some years back. Who could forget her slowly walking into their living rooms fresh from the surf to shore, the camera capturing her poise, beauty and perfectly proportioned tanned body in a wet bikini that glistened in the bright sunlight? Each of those men who watched that commercial time and again knew exactly why the guy in the ad on the beach with his girl got the bucket of water over his head. Well, this omnipresent Chinese was waiting for someone that afternoon in the lobby. She was the epitome of an Oriental beauty. Clay disliked the opinion he had of her but she was, doubtlessly, a very high-priced whore awaiting her millionaire yachtsman or/and Singapore businessman to arrive and whisk her away from view. And it just may have been that British Colonel, with the swagger stick, who just missed a glimpse of her as they circled the lobby again and again. It would be a shame if the two failed to meet.

Clay hated to leave the lobby but went to the front portico and got a cab. A tremendous thunderstorm developed as his cab headed for the airport. On his way out of the hotel, he rounded a corner of the registration desk and physically bumped into John Kenneth Galbraith, famed author, educator, diplomat.

What a huge man! Clay thought. In the early 1960's, he was the U.S. Ambassador to India.

On the second floor of the Singapore Airport was a good looking Chinese restaurant and Clay tried the soup, rice and tea.

Met by two staffers in Bangkok after the two hour flight from Singapore, they briefed Clay with the latest info on the annual flood in progress. Many parts of old Siam's capital were under two feet of water.

His scheduled army hotel was closed and so he was deposited at the First Hotel. One look at it and he shuddered to think what the Second Hotel would be like. Anyway, he was provided with a schedule for the next few days. While heavy, as most stops had been, this was the end of the string of official functions since Hong Kong. He would soon be on his own, halfway around the world and headed home.

Next morning, there were three and a half hours of meetings with top personnel. A lunch in the downstairs cafeteria was rushed to enable Clay to accompany many of the embassy staff to attend a very special observance at a huge Buddhist Temple: to witness the annual offering of gifts of cloth for robes, by the King's representative, for the monks.

The setting was in much splendor. Five embassy cars were required to take the Americans to the temple and all arrangements, to control traffic and stage everything properly, impressed Clay. It was not unlike a Presidential visit to a Sunday morning worship at a church in Washington, D.C.

A large section on one side of the interior of the temple was to seat all participants and guests to one of the most important events of the year. As Clay took his seat, the entire area in the center of the temple was then filled with orange-robed monks seated cross-legged on the floor. There may have been a hundred and the chants they intoned were fascinating in the interior of the temple and reverberated to the lofty ceiling of the structure. While it was a tie and coat affair for guests and visitors, mercifully there were large electric fans that sought to cool onlookers.

To Clay, the most moving event of the ritual was for him to be invited to come forward and offer one of the bundles of material and food, from a large table, to a monk. It was a very high honor for an American to be asked to be a participant in the ritual. For those few minutes, in utter silence, Clay was, by extension, the King of Siam's representative. He was very near tears as he handed the bundle to a monk, who stood before him and received the King's offering. The whole ceremony was rather short, but one that Clay would remember and cherish for a very long time. As the guests left the temple, they retrieved their shoes left at the doors outside. Very fortunately, Clay's socks had no holes.

A man named James H. W. Thompson, an American who had lived in Thailand since 1945, was born in Greenville, Delaware, in 1906. An architect by trade, he was assigned to the Office of Strategic

Services in World War II and went to Asia and finally
to Thailand where he remained after discharge on
V-J Day. He became interested in the commercial
possibilities of Thai silk and founded the Thai Silk
Company, Ltd. as the managing director. The products produced were handwoven and became a luxury
item in the world. His interest in Thai architecture
and art led to construction of his home on a klong,
the waterways famed in Bangkok, and an art collection of note. In 1967, Thompson disappeared on
holiday in the northern Malaysian resort of the
Cameron Highlands and not a clue to his fate exists
to date. As a very special gift, Clay was given a rare,
red silk-covered book by his embassy escort officer
concerning the Thompson home and art collection.
Now, here was a most remarkable man, thought
Clay, worthy, certainly, as an item on his quest list.
The disappearance of Thompson remained a mystery and intrigued Clay. He cherished the silk-covered book housed in the library of his Georgetown
townhouse. Every time Clay saw it on a coffee table
in his library, he was reminded of the myriad of
stories that had circulated throughout the Department of State, the Central Intelligence Agency and
the National Security Agency, not the least of which
was the probability that Thompson, an American spy
during World War II, had remained a spy for the CIA
and met his end because of it. Clay had long known
of the case and Thompson's mysterious disappearance. And Clay knew that Thompson's unknown fate
ranked up there in the rare company and notoriety
with that of Amelia Earhart, who also disappeared

in the Western Pacific and became a legend. Talk about a spy and/or a mystery thriller for one of "Win"'s movie script writers! Clay seemed to stand a little taller as he savored the strange story of one James H. W Thompson. And, wouldn't you know, Clay thought, that his escort officer, who presented him the valuable book, was a Jim Thompson?

Clay was fascinated by the klongs, or canals, of Bangkok that made it the Venice of Indo-China. The flooding in Bangkok, while an annual event, was then made worse by the unusually high tides at that time of year and the multi-pronged problems of the ocean, the klongs and the Chao Phyra River. Clay was told that the flooding he witnessed was the worst in thirty-three years. The crest was expected in a few days. But, already Clay's movements around the city were limited by standing water in many areas.

Clay observed an interesting fact to note in his journal that had nothing to do with his work schedule or the quest: the circumference of the earth was 24,902 miles. He was 12,451 miles from Washington, D.C., half way around. The only way he could have been further away would have been as an astronaut in space, an extra 200 miles straight up over Bangkok. Yes, the fact was that Clay was something of a trivia nut. In the lower grades, he gathered what he called "Little-known facts about the Presidents of the U.S." He gave it up when he got to college. But he had dozens of notebooks on Presidents and included such data as which President had the most pairs of trousers!

The flood went on for the next day or two. Clay was on an island at times in his hotel. From his dinner table, he could see the sea of water for blocks. Traffic was moving, but every passing car sent the water over curbs to store fronts along the street. Without the service of an embassy car, he would wade.

At his table one evening, there were four white orchids, with purple centers, in a vase. While he liked certain Thai dishes, it wasn't unusual for him to order Italian spaghetti or Chinese. He did have some free time away from embassy types to ease up, read a book or sit in the lobby and observe his surroundings.

One evening, however, some embassy staff took him to dinner at the Erawan Hotel's Le Chalet. Wonderful beef and a flaming banana sundae. Everything in that part of the world seemed so exotic to him: food, flowers and even the flooding itself gave his visit an unusual touch that caught all his senses. And a trip on the klongs would always be a special remembrance of Bangkok. It came the day before he was to depart the city and head toward Europe.

That morning, in the lobby as he awaited a car, a very young man, maybe fourteen or so he guessed, sat down at the grand piano and played beautifully. The lad did "My Way" and "Blue Moon," both well-done. What sounds filled the lobby before 8 A.M.!

At a klong, his car met some embassy staff who had hired a boat to traverse the klongs and enjoy a lunch on board that lasted until early afternoon. Clay had never seen so many boats and so many

different kinds, but mostly long, narrow and sleek
ones propelled by motors that appeared to be too
large, but that moved the crafts at a very high speed.
Neighborhoods built along the klongs were now
awash with the flood, but life went on. People were
seen washing clothes to hang on poles near their
wooden homes, swimming and bathing in the brownish, moving water. And along the klongs were many
wats or Buddhist shrines.

As the swift boats moved in both directions on
the klongs, you could imagine that whole families or
just single passengers were being transported, as if
by taxis without wheels, to various parts of Bangkok. Some of the outboard motors were huge in
comparison to the width and length of the boats,
most of which were with canopies and some with
multi-colored hulls. Many looked like elongated ca-
noes. Most of the very fast boats encountered on the
klongs had those large motors and tiny blades on
long shafts. It is probable that such motors were
developed in the area to master the navigation of the
winding klongs with speed, but also a sensitive ma-
neuverability. Clay learned there would be boat
races the week after he had to leave.

And there were also long lines of covered boats
encountered that were pulled along the klongs like
freight trains without rails. Many smaller boats had
oars and wobbled precariously when they were
struck by swift wakes from the speeding motorboats.
And there were also beautiful, enclosed, in-board
motor powered boats, not unlike the ferry boats that
serviced Puget Sound in Washington State, Admi-

ralty Inlet and the Strait of Juan de Fuca adjacent
to Vancouver Island, British Columbia, Canada.

But, perhaps the highlight of the outing on the
klong waters was the view, closeup, of two golden,
dragon-like-headed boats under cover at the Royal
Barge National Museum. One could easily imagine
those slender, splendid crafts, with strong rowers at
the oars, bearing the ancient Kings of Siam on the
klongs midst splendor with the mission to visit other
islands in the vast waterways. They would bear all
the trappings of early travels of similar luxury ships
that plied the waters of the Nile in Egypt in a bygone
era.

Clay was scheduled to take a Pan Am flight out
at 3 A.M. the morning after his birthday. He would
miss the sight of orange-robed monks walking down
the streets since dawn and each seemed to be loaded
down with food and offerings, including flowers.
They never begged. And he'd remember his visit to
that Buddhist Temple and the King's Representative
who was resplendent in a white uniform with gold
braid and ribbons.

With the tragedy of the flood, the embassy work,
the exotic flowers and social events, the trip on the
klongs, the Thai business types mostly educated in
the U.S., the wats, the monks, the world of old Siam
on his mind, it was no surprise to Clay that something would befall him en route to the airport very
early that morning of his departure. And, of course,
it did.

After a farewell dinner at an embassy
employee's home, Clay's driver took him by his hotel

to get his luggage. He was in the relative quiet of the lobby when he opened his birthday gift from Jamie, having carried it halfway around the globe. It was a pair of Pierre Cardin cufflinks with three intertwined gold bands, each of four strands, with the shape of them not unlike the globe he circled. He removed the ones he wore and replaced them with the new.

Luggage in the car and the decision made to go to the airport early so as not to make for such a long day for his driver, they pulled away from the hotel as water sprayed the sidewalks from the streets. It was near 10 P.M. and he'd have a long wait for his flight but he didn't mind. Once again, old habits controlled his decision of being early, even very early, rather than late to the airport. And, for good reason: the car stalled about twelve kilometers from the airport and the driver was able to coast from the flooded highway to a safe shoulder of the road in the pitch blackness of the night. The driver bounded out of the car, raised the hood and, of course, not only had the distributor cap gotten wet with water, but the driver had no cloth to dry it off.

"Take this!" Clay said as he took out an Irish linen, brand new handkerchief from his suit pocket.

"Sir..."

"Take it!" Clay replied over the din of the rain and passing traffic. Great Caesar! he thought.

What a hell of a place to be stranded in rain that then became a downpour! Fortunately, the driver used the handkerchief successfully to dry the inside

of the distributor cap and wipe around the spark-
plugs.

Confidently, the driver then closed the hood, got
into the car, turned the key in the ignition and the
motor came to life with a comforting roar as the
driver gunned the accelerator to complete the drying
job.

"Here you are, Mr. Stevenson," the driver said
as he started to pass the soggy, grease-stained handkerchief back.

"Keep it. Toss it on the floor up there and let's
go."

It would have been one hell of a long trek, with
luggage, had the blasted car failed to start. Clay was
glad he always carried a spare handkerchief. It must
have been from his Boy Scout days and the creed,
"Be Prepared."

Once ensconced in the Pan Am lounge, happy in
the knowledge that his luggage to check in was
downstairs ready for his flight some hours hence, he
had his flight bag and briefcase with him. The
lounge was like, "once you've seen one you've seen
them all," and had davenports...or were they
couches, Chesterfields or sofas?..., radio, TV and
stocked beverage mixes in an ice box. While he seldom took a drink after dinner and at that late hour
of near midnight, it was the last half-hour of his
birthday and he selected a miniature of Johnnie
Walker, Red Label, all fifty milliliters of it, put in a
bit of bottled water and leaned back to make a silent
toast to another birthday, a successful business trip
for the Department, a mental list of items for the

quest, the start of a leisurely four or five day trip to Paris, to Jamie for such a thoughtful gift, and...to a happy semi-vacation trip via New Delhi, Istanbul, Athens, Rome and thence to Dulles after a non-de-planing stop in Paris. He was rather anxious to get to his townhouse in Georgetown in Washington, D.C., his own familiar bed for the first time in nearly a month and, hopefully, a rendezvous, somehow and somewhere, with Jamie.

When he had made his multiple toasts and sa-vored his favorite scotch, his thoughts passed fleet-ingly to his conference sessions in Hong Kong, and the typhoon, the visits to Seoul, Tokyo, Manila, Sin-gapore and Jakarta and it all made a quilted image of the peoples and lands he had visited in such a short time. The emotions he had experienced, from the sensual touching to the sights, sounds, odors of half a world began to mesh, one into another and another until the whole, the pleasure and pain, be-came almost one. Sorrow and joy often overlapped and Clay was not sure which came first or became the other. It was a long roller coaster ride, all 12,451 miles of it, and Clay was unaware of what the same distance home would hold for him. With all official State duties behind him, the sorting out of some past quest items and those still to be encountered, he took what relaxation he could capture with relish. It had been an arduous trip and even more was just ahead. He knew, as he waited at the airport, that it was best not to know the future and what it would hold, for one could not rely on even one day at a time, but only every second into an unknown tomorrow. Just then, it was midnight, and he'd always remember his birthday in Bangkok.

It was just after 1 A.M. when someone knocked on the door of the Pan Am Lounge where Clay waited. He had leaned his head back on the davenport and dozed. The knock caused him to open his eyes immediately.

"Yes?"

"May I enter, Mr. Stevenson?"

"Who are you, Sir?"

"The Pan Am Bangkok Manager."

"Very well. Come in."

A bespectacled, middle-aged man, with a respectable bow to a special passenger on a Pan Am flight, introduced himself as a Walter Wenke.

"Hello, Mr. Wenke," Clay said and stood.

"Oh, please be seated, Mr. Stevenson. I do regret this intrusion at this hour."

"I can only imagine your visit is urgent and, even if it wasn't, it would be my pleasure to make your acquaintance. Your courtesy of this Lounge is appreciated."

"We know the importance of a bit of comfort on a long trip."

"Please have a chair, Mr. Wenke. Would you care for a beverage?"

"I'll sit, thank you, but I need nothing to drink. Mr. Stevenson, I received a call just minutes ago to contact you. The call came from the American Embassy in Bangkok and had been relayed from your embassy in Managua, Nicaragua."

"Nicaragua?"

"Yes, Sir. I have written on this sheet of paper the information passed to me by your local embassy staff."

"Yes..."

"It seems that a small Costa Rican airline plane crash-landed just hours ago in Nicaragua, in, yes,...Bluefields," as he referred to his notes.

"Bluefields?"

"Yes. The message from the American Embassy in Managua was that you were to be contacted here, this morning, on behalf of a Mr. and Mrs. Travis Goodson."

"My God! They are personal friends of mine! Were they killed?"

"No, sir. But they are being held by some small rebel forces in the southern and eastern part of Nicaragua and a ransom has been set for their safe release to American authorities in Managua."

"Can I get a long-distance line on this phone, Mr. Wenke?"

"Yes."

Clay picked up the phone and called the embassy duty officer in Bangkok, first.

"Good morning, the American Embassy, Bangkok."

"Yes...are you the duty officer?"

"Ben Wallace, sir, yes."

"Ben, this is Clay Stevenson at the Bangkok airport. We met in the last few days."

"Yes, Mr. Stevenson, of course."

"Ben, I've just been told by the Pan Am Manager here that a plane crash-landed in Nicaragua."

"Yes. I just called Mr. Wenke because we received in our communications' room an urgent call from Managua on behalf of a Mr. and Mrs. Travis Goodson."

"I know, Ben, I know. And they are being held by rebels in the southeast for ransom?"

"$20,000."

"I've heard. Why in hell doesn't Embassy Managua pay the sum out of their contingency funds and be done with it?"

"I'm told, Mr. Stevenson, that the rebel leader wants to make the worldwide news media aware of his military and political objectives and the only way for him to accomplish his goal is to see that his demands go all the way up to the Secretary of State."

"Well, why in hell didn't they pay?"

"Because of the series of rebel demands, other than money, for the Goodsons."

"Like...?"

"Certain arms and ammunition, including land-to-air missiles."

"Are you on a secure phone, Ben?"

"I am."

"Well, I'm not!"

"You are, Mr. Stevenson. We did some special routing to get you a clear line at the Lounge."

"Great Caesar! Wonderful. Congrats to communications, Bangkok, Ben!"

"Yes, sir."

"So, we need to reach the Secretary of State. Is he in Washington, D.C.?"

"Moscow."

"Can you reach our embassy in Moscow and get the secretary on the line...and on a secure phone, Ben?"

"I'll turn communications loose on it now, sir."

"Call me back, Ben, the minute you set up the phone relay."

"Of course." Both parties hung up.

"Would you like that drink now, Wenke?"

"Scotch on the rocks, please," Wenke said, as he removed his breast pocket handkerchief and wiped the perspiration from his brow and neck under his chin.

"What do you think of international diplomacy now, Mr. Wenke?"

"Amazed and gratified that you are seemingly able to work miracles."

"Hardly, but we try," Clay said and leaned back on the davenport. He opened another miniature, but didn't pour.

In ten minutes, at the most, Clay grabbed the phone before the first ring ended.

"Hello!" he said, loudly.

"I hear you plain and clear, Clay, on this secure phone. You needn't shout."

"Who in hell is this?"

"I'm the Secretary of State of the United States of America."

"Mr. Secretary, a thousand pardons. I imagined it would be embassy personnel in Moscow. I'm sorry, sir."

"I understand it is early in the morning in Bangkok. What is the problem, Clay?"

"It concerns some personal friends, a Mr. and Mrs. Travis Goodson, who survived a crash-landing in Nicaragua, but are being held for ransom in the southeastern part of the country by rebels with demands, also, for arms on a sophisticated shopping list."

"I have been briefed on all that, Clay."

"Is some movement underway to resolve this problem, then, Mr. Secretary?"

"There is not, Clay."

"Not?"

"Negative. You know the position of the United States regarding not only terrorists, but ransom demands from whatever source. I have no reason to think that policy will change in the near future."

"And you will not go to the President to get authority to resolve this case?"

"That is correct. I can not and will not."

"Thank you, Mr. Secretary."

"Goodnight, Clay."

Clay poured the opened miniature into his glass. Wenke went to the nearby counter in the lounge and offered some water from a bottle to Clay.

"Thanks, Wenke. I've got to keep a clear head on this one."

He picked up the phone and got Ben at the Embassy.

"Clay, here, Ben."

"You got to the Secretary?"

"Yes, and no dice."

"Next step?"

"Ben, get me the President of the United States."

Within half an hour, Clay had the President on Air Force One, headed for Colorado Springs for a speech to the U.S. Air Force Academy cadets.

"Mr. President?"

"Yes, Clay. This is the President."

"My call concerns an aircraft crash in Nicaragua..."

"I've been briefed, Clay. I have talked with the Secretary of State, now in Moscow, and have advised him to proceed with a special and new contingency plan, of which you are fully aware, to secure the release of the Goodsons by a bit of subterfuge. I won't go into details, but the Goodsons will be released to Managua embassy staff within the hour and the rest of the plan needn't concern you now. Good piece of work, Clay, to move on this over the Secretary's statement to you of our terrorism and hostage policy. Goodnight, Clay, and enjoy Athens!"

"Good-day, Mr. President."

ELEVEN

While Tegucigalpa in Honduras was charming, and El Salvador offered coastal scenes on the eastern Pacific and relaxation on sunny beaches, Travis and Ainsley stayed for only short visits before they moved on to Guatemala.

They had determined that it would be perhaps the last stop in Central America before a few days in Yucatan, Mexico, and then to Washington, D.C.

"Travis, it is so wonderful to be alive and have all the horror of the crash-landing in Nicaragua and our ingenious rescue behind us."

"You can say that again, love. I have passed the stage to need the arm sling and the X-rays in Nicaragua showed no broken ribs for you."

"You can't imagine how great it felt to get that tape off and my ribs only minimally wrapped for a while. It probably took longer to get the black, sticky stuff from the tape off my middle and back than it did to lose the pain of bruised ribs. My chest took a while to clear and lungs to get back to normal and, you know, Travis, I still feel a grit of sand in my mouth and around my teeth once in a while?"

"You had lots of sand in you on the beach at Bluefields, that's for sure."

"I'll never forget that miserable cart ride, but it was the only way to get me out. Oh, I cried, Travis, at the thought of leaving you behind, chained by a leg in that miserable clinic."

"Well, we seem to go over all that every day."

"I'd really like to know how Clay was able to extricate us from that rebel trap. I imagine he had phone lines buzzing!"

"I just realized, Ains, that we ain't got no goodies for 'Win'."

"What language for a specialist in international law! Well, I'll tell you what we do have: not only our lives, but a plot for a thrilling drama about an air crash, capture and rescue that would make not only a great movie, starring us, of course, but a film made for television, like HBO."

"Agreed. There would be big bucks realized from that adventure if it even was only a book. You used to be an editor, a journalism major, my dear. You could write such a book."

"But, remember, all the things we bring back at the end of the thirty-day quest period, become the property of 'Win', so don't forget that."

"But who could write a better tale than you, who lived it, not some hack writer in Hollywood who couldn't find Nicaragua on a map with both hands! A first-hand account would doubtlessly be better than a second- or third-hand book, that's for damn sure."

"Hungry?"

"Starving."

"Local food market or air-conditioned dining room in our hotel?"

"Surprise me."

At breakfast those several mornings, both Ainsley and Travis developed a taste for fresh papaya with a squeeze of lime, toast sans butter, and *cafe con leche*. In some areas they traveled, and, if they had some concern for the milk as to pasteurization, then it was *cafe negro*, black.

"Though it is lunchtime, Travis, I'm going to ask for papaya, toast and *cafe con leche*. We missed a few breakfasts in Nicaragua."

"I could have eaten all that vegetation our crash-landing ripped down when I had that chain around my leg and you obviously gone. It was hungerville!"

"And sad?"

"Very sad without you, Ains."

"Travis, you have started to call me 'Ains'. I rather like it."

"In that hulk of a plane there out in the surf, I just thought it would save time. We didn't have much time to play with."

In Nicaragua after the rescue of Travis and Ainsley, they were told at the embassy that all of the other passengers and the two-man crew were killed in that crash-landing. Many were drowned in the surf, some by trees tearing into the plane's fuselage as it plowed into the jungle, short of the beach.

"I'll be very pleased to hear you say 'Ains' from now on, anytime the urge strikes you. But, I'll still call you 'sweetheart', Travis. You're such a dear."

"Papaya good?"

"Wonderful!"

"How is the *leche*?"

"Pure as the driven snow or the cow that gave it. Fresh and so sweet."

"I have a notion, Ains, that, if our story is told or written, and you should write it while it is still as fresh in memory as that milk, we could offer it up as one item. And, who knows, it may outshine the lists developed by Rog and Clay."

"Okay by me, sweetheart," Ains said, "but I can't write it before the list is due! We'll just put down...'a book to be written on the high adventure of a plane crash, capture, held as hostages by rebels and our escape.'"

"Fine."

TWELVE

From Brugge to Brussels, Belgium, and thence to Paris by train, Rog and Brandy were awed and thrilled by the size and beauty of the City of Light. With memorable sights of their swing around England, to Scotland and Belgium fresh in their minds, they were eager to experience the many places of reknown in historic Paris.

They found a room in a small hotel on the West Bank of the Seine with a spectacular view to the

Eiffel Tower and then took a 360 degree look at Paris from the top landing of the steel structure. They could see Notre-Dame, the great Cathedral; the twisting Seine River that snaked through the city like a giant serpent; the Arch of Triumph, a landmark commissioned by Napoleon to honor his army; the Louvre and the impressive gardens; Versailles, with its palace and magnificent grounds; the Elysèe on the famed Champs Elysèes; and, in addition, Rog took countless photos of the huge residential buildings and downtown shopping centers.

Once they had their bearings from such a great height, they selected those attractions, in no certain priority, for they were determined to see them all.

They were struck by the proximity of their hotel to the tourist areas and their large room on the ground floor was very attractive. The first evening back at the hotel, after walking, boating and dining out, the room itself held an item that caught Rog's eye immediately. The marble fireplace, while not needed in September, had a brass peacock ornament in front of it that was more than for ornamental purposes. It was designed, no doubt, to radiate heat outward when in use. It was, perhaps, also a fire screen.

"Brandy, what do you think of that brass fan-like item in front of the fireplace?"

"It would seem rather practical on a cold evening to warm guests. It is quite beautiful, too, as it now stands there. Do you find it of merit for the quest?"

"I'm not just sure, but I wanted your opinion and you noted its practicality immediately."

"I've seen them in the States, it seems, but I could be mistaken. Though many fireplaces in America are now gas heated, the reflector value of those brass feather-like, moveable blades should not be overlooked even though many regular fireplaces have been modified."

"Good observations. Do we have gin in our baggage?"

"We do and I'll get ice at the front desk and fix us a happy hour cocktail. Would you object?"

"I'd be delighted."

Both were a bit weary from the events of the first day and they needed to rest and be refreshed for the next.

They were up and around near 9 A.M. and took a taxi to Montmartre, where sidewalk artists paint and sell their canvases to tourists. Brandy bought one which became a reminder to them of a typical Parisian street scene for their Baltimore home. It was most colorful and worth the price she paid. Rog was pleased with it, too.

They took their wine that day at a colorful sidewalk cafe and watched the people passing by, not all tourists by any means. After lunch at a quaint restaurant near Notre-Dame, they took a taxi to Versailles, the court of French kings before the French Revolution. But twelve miles from Paris, the landscape gardener, Andrè Le Note, created the most perfect of formal French gardens. The Hall of Mirrors was the setting for the Treaty of Versailles at the end of World War I, and in the early 1800's, it was the site of a museum of French history. Massive gardens were to the west of the pink and cream stone palace.

"I hate to say it, Brandy, but we should soon make final reservations for our return home," Rog said over dinner near their hotel.

"I miss our little brood," Brandy admitted.

"So do I. Do we have enough gifts to please them all?"

"I'm sure."

"Do we have a few ideas, also, for the quest that we think will stand up against those brought by Travis and Clay?"

"Well, we are fairly set on a bed and breakfast scheme and on those huge Bath Buns. I still say that, if Thomas' English Muffins were a lucrative import for the American market, those buns could also be rather well received."

"Agreed. And, perhaps, that brass fireplace reflector. I like it a great deal."

At the huge De Gaulle Airport the next day, Rog and Brandy, happier together than they had been in a very long time and filled with joy with Brandy's turn for the better in the course of the trip, it seemed certain that the return to Baltimore, the medical practice, the children, would lighten the weight that had been on their shoulders for years.

THIRTEEN

It seemed an eternity for Clay, as he had waited several hours, before leaving Bangkok. When he was in the Pan Am plane that would take him to Athens, he had a feeling of euphoria as he began the swing around the back side of the earth. While he departed in the pitch blackness of very early morning before sunrise, he had an unforgettable experience. The weather was clear as a bell from Bangkok west and, for a time, the Big Dipper was balanced on the wingtip outside his window. What a remarkable sight it was! The whole starry universe was perhaps the brightest he had ever seen it, save some brilliant nights in Wyoming and Idaho.

He reflected on some news he had heard in Bangkok before he was airborne: there were comments directed to him that his departure was just in time. All state and government employees were encouraged to take time off from work, schools were closed for a week and the river was to rise even more. If it rained, the situation would be very serious.

Dawn in Delhi was a delight. The huge plane was refueled and, in near perfect weather for optimal vision of the ground areas, Clay saw the coastal city of Karachi, Pakistan, Afghanistan, Iran, Iraq before the next stop in Istanbul, Turkey. He had never seen so much desert and barren mountains before and all were lands he would never walk on in his lifetime. There was just too much on the globe to see and experience.

Before arrival in Istanbul, Clay recalled his conversation with the President on Air Force One as that special plane headed for Colorado. Clay thought: he had gone about as high up as anyone had gone to get a Presidential decision on Travis and Ainsley Goodson. He tried to imagine the terror his friends had experienced in a crash-landing in a jungle and the Caribbean off Nicaragua and how pleased he was to have been instrumental in getting them released by rebels. As far as the quest was concerned, he had made a Michael Jordan "miracle basket" for a player, like Travis, on the opposite team, but Clay was glad. The Goodsons would have done as much for him.

The airport stop in Istanbul conjured up all the mystique about an ancient city which, to Clay, had always left a sinister connotation in his mind. It was interesting, however, to order coffee in the terminal and observe the waiters who carried cups of strong Turkish coffee to passengers.

Clay had noted in his journal some trivia of interest to him: the flight from Bangkok to New Delhi, three hours and forty minutes; an hour and a half to Karachi; and five hours to Istanbul. And that coffee in the airport at Istanbul was carried on two balanced trays that looked every bit as if the waiters carried the scales of legal justice!

An Air France flight got Clay to Athens and the Hilton where he could barely see the Acropolis. Next morning, he moved to the downtown Astor Hotel. It was a clear, sunny day.

Clay ordered a half bottle of white wine, Achaia Clauss, domestic, asparagus soup and a bit of feta cheese. Delectable! From the rooftop restaurant at the Astor, recommended to Clay by someone back on his trail of travel, Jakarta he thought, the Acropolis was almost touchable! Spectacular!

He took a cab to the site of the Parthenon on a hill which was the Acropolis. He hired a guide to walk him around the ancient site. He wanted one of the numerous marble chips scattered over the entire area. Just one. But Clay finally decided that if every visitor to the Acropolis had the same urge, not only the chips, but the entire remains would eventually be carried away. The British had, years earlier, taken one of the twelve columns of the Athena Temple, made in the form of a maiden, to London! That was bad enough.

Athens reminded Clay of San Francisco, also built on seven hills as Athens. The brightness, from so much white of the mass of buildings, glistened and sparkled.

Next morning, Clay was in Rome. The chimes near his hotel rang out. Had he wanted to write a horror story, he would have used his old hotel, The Commodore, as the setting.

He took a bus tour to the Pantheon and St. Peter's. He saw the Pietà. Next morning, it was to the Colosseum and the Catacombs. At lunch, he had real Italian spaghetti in tomato sauce and a glass of Chianti Ruffino, one of the finest, according to an Italian Clay had met years earlier in Washington, D.C. As he ate, a waiter wheeled a cart by his table that bore a whole roast pig with an apple in its mouth. It was at the Ristorante Scoglio di Frisio.

Clay had to note another trivia: in Rome, there were twenty-four bridges over the Tiber River, four of them from the days of the Romans. The city dated from 753 B.C. and, though the Colosseum was memorable to Clay, it was formerly covered in white marble, while now it was mostly brick work. The structure became a quarry for building materials for homes.

Clay's flight from Rome stopped in Paris, but he didn't leave the plane. He had crossed the Alps; he saw Mount Blanc. It was eight hours from Paris to

Dulles and when he saw that modernistic building of the future, he knew he was back home.

FOURTEEN

"Do I understand that September 30 at midnight is your deadline for receipt of those lists from the three men?" Senator Hudson Blake of Nevada asked.

"That is the date and it is fast approaching," "Win" answered. "Roger Thomas, Travis Goodson and Clay Stevenson were the three who accepted my invitation to search for items of excellence. Two of them, Thomas and Goodson, took their wives. Clay is single and traveled alone around the world."

"Good Heavens, he must be exhausted or will be on his return," Hud commented.

"He has returned, I'm told, by an associate. Just back into Dulles."

"And the other two?"

"Both are scheduled to be in any day now, one to Dulles and the other, perhaps, to Washington National Airport."

"And another question, 'Win', have you arranged a time certain with Judge Brooks to receive those three lists from you for study? Will his court calendar allow him the proper time to deliberate on the merits of those listed items?" The Senator hesitated, "You know, 'Win', I wouldn't think of telling you how to run this quest, as you call it. It is only because of my Senate schedule and my committee obligations that prompt me to make these inquires of you so that I can be sure I have a clear slate when my specific role comes into play. You do understand, 'Win'?"

"Of course, Senator. Both the Judge and you will need some time, say a day or two, to reach the conclusion of your inputs, so as you both can then proceed on Senate and Court business. Yes, I've made a determination that I have sent to Judge Brooks in a letter."

"Sounds good."

"I'll contact each of the three men before the September 30, midnight, deadline and have their lists hand-delivered to Judge Brooks in Wilmington, Delaware, on October 1. So, my deadline of September 30 is firm and the Judge is prepared to commence his work on them on the evening of the 1st."

"Now, 'Win', just a few words on my responsibilities to my 'special contacts' in Las Vegas. They have agreed to look at the results of the quest not later than October 5, and, I suspect even that date may be moved up a day or two to respond to others, most of whom are overseas, who have put certain limitations on actions in Las Vegas. So, it is very obvious, to you, to me, to the Judge, to my men in Las Vegas and their 'unnamed' contacts overseas, that results will be forthcoming, give or take a day or two, by October 5. That date must be the very outside limit, otherwise the whole arrangement, on the States' side and overseas, too, will collapse. Too much has gone into our strategic plan to allow for any slippage. I'm certain you and I understand each other on those points."

"Perfectly," "Win" answered.

"Have you also considered the ways and means to make sure that those three men, Thomas, Goodson and Stevenson, will not, I repeat, not be privy to the end result of their lists and my role particularly in this whole scheme, rather...business venture?" Hud queried. "It is an absolute must that my name not be divulged in any way, shape or form to the three men, the Judge, his employees and any others who may be on the outer fringes, of never knowing my role."

"I give my assurance," "Win" responded. "I might just add, Senator, that steps will be taken to allow no leakage of what we have discussed to the two wives nor any girl friends or current paramours of Clay Stevenson. I have men ready to monitor Ste-

venson and the other 'players,' Thomas and Goodson."

"Well," the Senator said as he walked to a cabinet near his desk, "how about a snort?"

"Please."

The two men clicked their lead crystal shot
glasses together, smiled and nodded to one another
and downed the bourbon.

"Want my secretary to ring Robert?"

"Thanks, no, Senator. He is just outside the Hart
Senate office Building door ready to drive me to
Bethany Beach immediately."

"Very well," the Senator said, moving away from
his desk to escort "Win" to the door, and, as all
politicians are wont to do, shook hands, and gave a
friendly pat on the back of his guest. It seemed to
work: to seal a deal or insure a vote.

FIFTEEN

"Hey, Mom! Dad!" Jimmy called out at Dulles International Airport as Rog and Brandy exited the door from U.S. Customs. Rosalie and Sue jumped up and down as they waved and shouted and were the first to run and greet their parents. Jimmy, the eldest, hung back, swinging the family car keys back and forth. His grandmother had decided to give him the responsibility to pick up the returning travelers and she would stay home. Jimmy had his driver's license and was the "big man" in the small welcom-

ing group for his folks. Brandy handed some pack-
ages to Rosalie and Sue and hugged them both. Rog
first shook hands, and then kissed Jimmy's cheek in
a bear-hug, and handed him his suitcase, while Rog
got the remainder of the luggage from the cart.

"How is Mother? Did she survive all of you?"

"Of course. She wouldn't let us do some of the
things we wanted to do because she didn't know if
we really had permission from you," said Rosalie.
Sue added an example or two, like going to a night
movie without her. "So," Sue said, "we watched television after our homework."

Rog put the suitcases down once away from the
doorway and other passengers hurrying out and
hugged both of the younger girls.

"Want me to drive, Dad?" Jimmy asked as they
went out the baggage room doors and headed for the
car in the parking lot.

"Son, I'd love to drive an American car on the
right side of the street. I'll drive. You drove the girls
here. I'll get you all home. Dads love to do that."

"O-k-a-y," Jimmy said, reluctantly.

"What did you bring us?" the girls asked in
unison.

"Each of you a pack of gum and Jimmy, two
packs, he's bigger," Rog said.

"Come on! What real presents?" Rosalie asked.

"Well," Brandy said, "I might be able to find a
thing or two in my carry-on when we get to the car."

"Goodie, goodie! What are they?" the girls
begged.

"When we get to the car you'll know. Do you know where the car is, Jimmy?" Brandy asked.

"Sort of."

"What?" said Rog. "If you can drive a car you should remember where you park it."

"I'll find it," he said.

And, after a few wrong rows and backtracking, the car was found and loaded.

"Wonderful to be home with all of you," Rog said, as he headed out of the lot.

"Can we make cookies tonight, Mom?" Sue asked.

"We'll see. Maybe."

The Goodsons found Merida on the Yucatan Peninsula too torrid and so left on the next available flight for Miami. They overnighted at the Fontaine-bleau Hotel on Miami Beach to escape Mexico and used it as a decompression chamber for a breather before flying out the next morning for National Airport in Washington, D.C.

At dinner in the beach-front hotel, they savored whole lobsters, flown in from Maine, no doubt, and took in plenty of ice water after so much bottled water in Central America.

"How are the ribs tonight?"

"On the menu or my body?" Ainsley answered.

"Body and they are not edible."

"Oh, fine. Still need a bit of wrap but, generally, okay. I still, despite the agony of a painful rib cage for so long, hardly believe that we were in a plane crash, Travis. You do know that the odds, we're told by the airlines, are about one in a million. Well, we caught one of those 'ones' in Bluefields, Nicaragua."

"And, I would suspect, Ainsley, that the odds for one to have an emergency appendectomy in Costa Rica are about one in a billion," Travis stated.

"How's the incision?"

"Looks like a Toonerville Trolley twisty track."

"What kind of a track?"

"Toonerville Trolley. Didn't you ever read the comics as a kid?"

"Dick Tracy. Not that one you read."

"Rog would know."

"About the comics?"

"The incision. I'll ask him."

"Not Rog. Ask your own doctor at your next appointment."

"We are survivors, Ains."

"I know. We may be met by press in D.C. if they know we're coming in tomorrow. The media needs news to be the media, you know."

"Well, if we are, don't give out too much data. You can mention your ribs and your sorrow at the loss of life. Just keep in mind that you may, and could, be the only one to write a good adventure book about the experience. In so many cases, sadly, no one lives to tell the tale."

"Only those little black boxes."

"Yeah."

"Travis, big time lawyers in a prestigious Washington, D.C. law firm don't say 'yeah'."

"Yeah? I'll bet Abe Lincoln as a lawyer and as President said 'yeah' anytime he wanted to say it."

"I've heard that same line from Brandy!"

SIXTEEN

"Please step into my office, Miss Greening," the Judge said on his intercom.

"Yes, Judge Brooks," Megan answered.

The United States Court House was located at 844 N. King Street in Wilmington, Delaware. The six-story building housed not only the Delaware District Federal Court, but also the United States

Internal Revenue Service offices. The Federal Court occupied the entire top floor.

Physically, the large courtroom was on one side of the center of the sixth floor, flanked on the north by the chambers of Judge Sumner Brooks, Sr. and, on the south, his private suite. The courtroom, the chambers and the suite were all wood-paneled. A large office next to his suite was a private office for his legal secretary and staff. And, on the opposite side of the suite, were the library and the private office of Megan Greening, his law clerk.

The United States Court House, Wilmington, was built in the 1980's under the Reagan Administration and was a showcase for modern Federal courts in the nation's judicial system and, while small compared to other Federal institutions in the United States, it fit Wilmington's needs as the second smallest state in the union. Both Brooks' legal secretary and law clerk had side doors directly connected to the Judge's private suite.

"Good Morning, Judge."

"Megan." The Judge was more likely to call her by her first name for she reminded him so much of a daughter, his only child. Outside the presence of others, he always called her Megan and, once in a great while, perhaps over lunch, Meg. She never considered calling him other than Judge or Judge Brooks. She had taken her law degree at Harvard, was a Wilmington native, where her father was a partner in a prestigious law firm that, one day, would consider her as a candidate for the firm, too. But, now, as Judge Brooks' law clerk, she was gaining invaluable experience with an eminent jurist, whose name had been on short lists of Presidents seeking possible appointees to the United States Supreme Court. Many in political and legal circles in the nation had predicted that Judge Brooks might get a nomination for the next vacancy.

"I have just received a letter from an acquaintance of mine, Mr. Winfield Agar, who had previously invited me to be helpful to him in examining some lists of recommendations regarding possible business ventures he and his colleagues may want to pursue. While my legal secretary and staff are hard at work, as you know, on preparing cases for the upcoming docket, I'm going to ask you to handle the legal research that may be entailed. Here is the letter just delivered by messenger from Winfield Agar down in Bethany Beach. As you will see, there is a time limit involved in which certain lists come to him and he will forward them on to me to make some sort of judgement as to the legal implications and general value of items that may be on those lists. It would be most helpful, Megan, because of the time limit he has requested, to ask you to research the legal ramifications before submitting them to me for a decision."

"I understand, Judge."

"And, Megan, your research papers are to be given only to me and their contents are not to be revealed outside these offices of the court. They are not to be turned over to my legal staff, but only to me."

"Yes, Judge. I will open a new research file re: this letter from Mr. Agar and all future communications from him."

"That is entirely satisfactory. One other thing, Megan. When your research file is not being utilized, I would ask you to see that it is locked in the safe in your office."

"Of course, Judge."

"When next we get a communication from Mr. Agar, I would like to see it forthwith before turning it over to you for action."

"Yes, Judge."

"I'm making a personal call now to the mail distribution rooms in this building to give them specific instruction to route all Agar correspondence to you, by hand, when received."

"Yes, Judge."

"Thank you, Megan."

Megan left his office by the side door from his private suite into her own office.

At her desk, she read the letter the Judge had given her from Mr. Agar and immediately opened a new file under the name of Winfield Randolph Agar, of Bethany Beach, Delaware, as requested by the Judge.

SEVENTEEN

At home in Baltimore, the day after their return from Europe, Brandy penned a few lines for Rog:
"Taxied up to Montmartre,
One painting caught my eye,
A reflection of old Paris,
To see it, brings a sigh."
Rog, glad to have Brandy's offering for his poem, wrote of Versailles:
"We walked the site Marie loved,

It was a kind of veld,
But it, nor she, could ever match,
The Queen, whose hand I held."

"Oh, Rog," Brandy said when she read the poem in its entirety, "it is lovely, so very beautiful. We should both treasure it in remembrance of our trip."

"I'll get it typed up, put it in an appropriate frame and hang it in our family room."

"Very good, Rog."

"Your several contributions, my love, are what makes the poem of special value to me. I hope you know, Brandy, how very much I enjoyed the trip with you. We are going to have to do another before long, maybe two or so a year. Would you like that?"

"Of course, but we must watch some expenses because a trip such as we just took dipped into our savings a bit. And, Rog, we must be ready to handle college educations for our three and you know how costs have escalated in recent years. And, too, we should get a computer in this house. I'm sure we all could benefit from it. But, then again, we five would almost have to take turns on it and you can imagine the problems that may follow."

Rog knew she was so right about funds not being as readily available as one might imagine, considering even the large practice Rog enjoyed at the clinic. And it took quite a bit of ready cash to buy the beach house in Middlesex. People almost took it for granted that doctors earned a great deal of money and some did. Not all, however. Some, like Roger, were really just beginning to enjoy a sizeable practice at the clinic and it took a lot of earlier savings to develop it, which had its own particular advantages, such as staff backing and financial support supplied by Johns Hopkins University Hospital.

And, too, there was a growing family, with three fine children, as the Thomas' off-spring. A budget was certainly a must for their household and it had evolved from small to quite large over more recent years.

Rog secretly cherished the strides made by Brandy on their trip. She even asked him, in London, or was it in Scotland? Scotland he thought. But, anyway, she asked him if he had brought her medication! He had, of course, and it raised his spirits to know that she was seeking the help she had so long refused. How wonderful! How very wonderful!

When Clay had completed the customs' ordeal and was about to catch a cab at the curb at Dulles on his return the day before Rog, a limo driver approached him and told him that a Jamie Agar was there to pick him up. She was full of surprises, Clay thought, as he turned over his luggage to the driver and, as the door was opened for him, he peeked in to see a smiling Jamie Agar.

"Welcome home, Clay," she said.

"So wonderful to see you," he said and got in.

"Don't frown, Clay. You looked worried," she said. "This is not the Agar limo. I rented it so that I could meet your flight."

"How thoughtful! I'm overwhelmed. How did you know?"

"I called the Asia Bureau at Main State and asked for your arrival date and flight. Don't worry. I pretended I was a reporter for the travel section of <u>The Washington Post</u> and sought an interview with you on your return from a trip around the world. No names were mentioned, except yours, and it may have even been your secretary who gave me the data I needed."

"I'm pleased you were so discreet," Clay said.

With the luggage stowed in the trunk, the driver got in, started the car and began to move the limo out of the loading areas at the terminal and it was soon on the access road to the city. It was after 6 P.M. and Clay suggested to Jamie that he be dropped off at his Georgetown residence rather than Main State.

"Perfectly agreeable," Jamie responded. "Perhaps you know a nice place in Georgetown where we could have a drink before going to your townhouse to deliver you and your luggage. Then I must meet Robert, my driver, and return to the beach. And be assured, Clay, I won't linger too long for I know you must be exhausted by that trip from Bangkok."

"Excellent plan and I concur. What is today, the 27 or 28, September? I've lost track."

"It is the 28th, Clay."

"I'll have a full day at the office tomorrow, debriefing, the 29th, and then I'll head to the beach that night or next morning. I have to give a lot of thought to my list and have it ready for 'Win' before midnight, the 30th."

"I want to wish you luck, Clay," and she leaned over toward him and kissed his cheek. He took her into his arms, kissed her and held her very tight.

It was early afternoon, on September 28th, when Travis and Ainsley arrived at Washington National Airport. They had guessed correctly: there were two television crews, channels 4 (NBC) and 7 (ABC) on hand at their arrival gate. Two or more reporters and photographers were also on hand from The Washington Times, The Washington Post and USA Today. They had cameras set up at an empty gate and waiting area across from the one into which the Goodsons emerged and they wasted no time in getting Travis and Ainsley in front of the cameras before the bombardment of questions began. There were at least half a dozen microphones hooked up into a bunch on the table, behind which the Goodsons were escorted and asked to sit down.

"Were you the only survivors?"

"Is it true you were treated badly by the rebels?"

"What was it like to be hostages?"

"How did you escape?"

Both Travis and Ainsley were somewhat confused by the rapid questions asked of them, many overlapped by another so that words became a tangle.

"Please, folks," Travis said, "please, please, one at a time. We'll do our best to accommodate all of you, but we need to hear the questions."

"Were there others survivors?"

"There were no others. We tried to locate some to assist but it all happened so quickly," Ainsley answered.

"Was the airplane crash in Guatemala or Costa Rica?"

"It was east of Managua near Bluefields in Nicaragua."

"Bluefields?"

"Yes, Bluefields."

"Did you know your rescuers were rebels at the time?"

"No, we did not."

"Do you intend to write a book?"

"We haven't given much thought, really, to anything except getting home and some rest."

"Where is home?"

"On Chesapeake in N.W. Washington, D.C."

"Have you been contacted by any Hollywood film studios?"

"We just arrived," Travis said. "We've talked to no one."

"Would you ever go back to Nicaragua after this horrific experience?"

"We probably would, yes," said Ainsley, who let Travis do most of the talking.

"You are an attorney in D.C.?"

"Yes."

"Which one, which firm?"

"Folks, thank you, but I'm sure you can appreciate the fact that we want to go home and get some
rest. So, excuse us, please, and thank you for meeting us," Travis said and stood up.

"The Post would like an exclusive interview this
afternoon at your home. Can you confirm that for
me?"

"Please. We must go. Please. Thank you."

They were escorted by a couple of Airport Security officers from the gate to luggage claim as most
of the reporters rushed along behind, ahead and
beside them, camera lights flashing all the way.

Senator Hudson Blake asked his secretary to
send his Administrative Assistant into his office.

"Yes, Senator," she answered.

Roscoe Manley excused himself from a constitu-
ent of the Senator's in his private office, knocked on
the Senator's door, and hurried in.

"Roscoe, I want you to take the next plane, or an
Air Force plane, whatever, to Vegas. I have a note in
this envelope I want hand delivered to...well, you
know the name of the man. Call me the minute you
deliver it and have my friend ready to get on the
phone with me. This is urgent, Roscoe."

"Yes, Senator."

"I'm in the midst of cocktails with some business associates, Jamie," "Win" said on the phone. "I'm in Rehoboth Beach and there is to be a late dinner here. Don't wait up for me, my dear. I must go," "Win" said and hung up the phone.

Jamie replaced the phone on its stand, crossed the room, and poured some Chevis Regal into a tall glass over ice and added some water from a silver pitcher on the wet bar. She looked out at the boiling surf from the mammoth window, the drapes opened widely near the end of the September day.

"Clay," said the Assistant Secretary of State for Asian Affairs, "that was an excellent briefing. You did a superb job in your country-hopping, and as well, of course, in Hong Kong. I have received many commendations on your behalf from that part of the world. And, as to K-123, it seems to have been well-received at all of our major embassies in the area. This special presentation you made, on the President's orders, was handled like the diplomatic expert you are and a credit to the Department's Foreign Service. You helped introduce a new, important and necessary Presidential policy in the Orient. It is a breakthrough in methods to combat national and/or international terrorism and remains highly classified. Thank you."

"Megan," Judge Brooks said as they sat in his private office, "I wanted you to understand one vital point that has changed since our last conversation regarding the opening of that new file on Winfield Agar, that's Winfield Randolph Agar."

"Yes, Judge. That is how I labeled it."

"Very good. The point I want to add is this: the lists sent here by Mr. Agar will not be hand-delivered as he originally advised me. Your FAX number has been given to Mr. Agar. Mr. Agar will doubtlessly fax some information directly to your office not only during the day of September 30, but also, perhaps, after midnight on October 1. Should I be available, and though I have a judicial association dinner that night, I may go to your office to check on incoming fax messages. I will put them, if any, in your safe for the night and you will check on the morning of October 1, at regular office hours, if any new messages arrived and properly log them in."

"I understand. I could even plan to have dinner in my office and be available should..."

"That won't be necessary, my child. Just look to arriving the next morning, as usual, and I will be in first thing to look at the file on the 1st."

"Fine, Judge."

As Megan closed his office door, the old Judge leaned back in his black leather chair. Megan, he thought, was so like his own daughter of twenty years ago, when last he saw her alive.

"Megan," he said aloud, "she was my law clerk, too. Her name, Megan, as you know, was Brenda."

"Rog, please don't drive so fast, dear," Brandy implored. "Traffic is dreadful!"

Rog didn't slow. He looked straight ahead at the night road, for oncoming lights were very bright on the wet pavement as the rain continued to pelt down.

"It is near eleven o'clock, Brandy, and we still have a ways to go to get to 'Win''s."

"I know, but..."

"I'll slow a bit, Brandy, but you know this is the 30th and the deadline is midnight. You try and relax and let me concentrate on driving. The staff meeting at Johns Hopkins lasted much later than we all anticipated. You were very patient to wait as you did. Sweetheart, do you have any misgivings about our list?"

"We've been all over this. The bed and breakfast and the Bath Buns seem just fine. We did our best."

"Yes, dear, I think we did our very best." He still wasn't really sure whether or not they should have dropped the brass fireplace radiator as he wrote out their list of two, only.

Clay drove his classic T-bird, hard top on, in the blinding rain and was over the Chesapeake Bay Bridges in normal time. In less than two hours, he should pull up into "Win"'s driveway. By his usual planning, delays en route included, he should arrive well before midnight. He felt for a moment like...no, not Cinderella, but Prince Charming, as the last hour approached.

Clay loved the T-bird. As the sound, well-tuned motor purred, he switched his thoughts to his list: one, the solid bar headlights for future cars; two, the smoke hoods, and he equated smoke hoods in fires with air bags in car crashes, and he had debated whether to list that item first or second; three, the white-haired Japanese gentleman he had observed in the Rose Room on his Tokyo stop en route to Hong Kong. He seemed to Clay to be a natural for a movie or a documentary film on the life of a Japanese Naval officer or a General, before, during and after World War II; and, four, the dice game. While he had a number of vivid remembrances of unusual experiences, the Hong Kong typhoon and including the Kisaeng dinner in Seoul, he settled on the dice game, another object, but worthy, he felt, for his list. He went over the four again and again as he drove, but, while he mentally tried to substitute something for one of the four, he couldn't believe the four could be cracked. So, he clung to his same four, and glanced at one of his thin briefcases, on the seat beside him, that held the list for "Win."

"Travis," Ainsley said at their beach house in Middlesex Beach, Delaware, "I feel about as naked this very minute as I did on that beach in Nicaragua a few days ago. I don't recall what I had on then, if anything, but I feel as, what's the saying, 'naked as a Jay-bird'?"

"That naked?"

"Yes."

"Why?"

"We ain't got no list for 'Win' tonight."

"Wives of lawyers in prestigious Washington law firms, don't say, 'we ain't got no.'"

"I don't give a damn!"

"Ains. Cool it! We have but one and it will be a winner: a story of survival in a steaming Central American jungle, captured by rebels or, better, bandits, escaped and lived to tell about it."

"It doesn't sound like enough. We put up $2000 for one item. Clay probably has a solid four and Rog, well, who knows. Maybe two or three, tops."

"Ains, it only takes one!"

"Yeah?"

"Wives of lawyers in prestigious Washington law firms, don't..."

"To hell with it!"

"Ains, save that line for the book."

The recipient of Senator Hudson Blake's hand-delivered letter knew exactly what to do. He caught the next plane for Wilmington, Delaware.

It was October 1. Promptly, at 9 A.M., Megan Greening arrived at her office. She unlocked her door, switched on the lights and saw the body of Judge Brooks, face down, a wound at the back of his head that had turned his snow-white hair to a matted-red. Megan's wall safe was open. All happened in seconds and Megan let out a loud, terrified scream that brought a building guard running into her office, as Megan fell in a faint and was sprawled on the floor.

EIGHTEEN

Senator Hudson Blake of Nevada had served for eighteen years in the United States Senate and, like so many before him, he determined that he would seek the nomination for President of the United States.

It was common knowledge that it required millions of dollars to conduct a nationwide campaign, what with the myriad of state primaries, to finance "blitz" television and radio commercials, and, if the

nomination was won, to expend even more legal
millions of dollars, taxpayers and private alike, not
to mention the "soft money" that national political
committees were allowed to collect from the giants
of corporate America and certain overseas businesses alike.

In order to meet his needs for money, he entered
into a "political" alliance with Winfield "Win" Randolph Agar, a millionaire businessman, who agreed
to join in the unofficial Hudson Blake campaign in
return for 50% of the funds collected, many illegally,
from overseas. To insure a massive infusion of dollars for Blake and himself, he devised the plan that
would be known as his worldwide treasure hunt. It
was in this "quest" that he offered a million dollars
in cash, deposited in the Baltimore Trust Company
bank in Bethany Beach, Delaware, to one of the
three men who took the challenge: Clay Stevenson,
Roger Thomas and Travis Goodson. He was quite
certain that those three talented and professional
men would dredge up contacts and ideas overseas
that would produce millions of dollars by domestic,
new overseas businesses and/or even those imported
into the United States. "Win" was fully aware that
Senator Hudson Blake was determined to raise
those huge amounts of money before the Congress of
the United States passed the needed and the well-
known Campaign Finance Reform legislation that,
among other things, would make certain "soft" national and overseas money, henceforth, officially
illegal. And that is why Agar set the thirty-day time
limit to cause the three men in the "game" to find

lucrative new business enterprises at the earliest possible date. It made the quest for Stevenson, Thomas and Goodson a race against time to win the prize, but they were unaware that Agar and Blake had a "deal."

On the night of September 30, with a midnight deadline for the three men to submit their lists to "Win", he was in Rehoboth Beach, Delaware, as he told Jamie, and he would not be in Bethany Beach to receive and fax the three lists to Judge Sumner Brooks, Sr. in Wilmington. Therefore, to keep Jamie from the truth of the whole scheme, he gave Juan, his trusted houseboy, the fax number of Megan Greening's office, phoned to "Win" by Judge Brooks himself, who was led to understand that "Win" would donate a respectable sum of money to him for his time entailed in selecting the winner of the million dollar prize.

With that all set up to his satisfaction, "Win", not in Rehoboth Beach for a late business night as he had told Jamie, was, instead, in Wilmington. There, "Win" learned that the Judge was to attend a judicial dinner and, would, in all probability, go to his Federal Building suite just after midnight to receive the three lists faxed to Megan's office and, rather quickly, make a decision among the three. The Judge had been asked to write a single name, on a blank sheet of paper, of which of the three men won the prize.

As it happened, the three men, Rog, Travis and Clay, delivered their lists personally to the Agar beach house north of Bethany Beach, well before midnight, September 30. Each was greeted by Juan and Jamie and she turned over each list to Juan, who had his instructions from "Win" regarding Megan Greening's fax number. He dutifully faxed them, each the moment they were in his hands.

Megan Greening, while the Judge had asked her not to go to her office on the night of the 30th, but on October 1, at her usual time, to read the faxes and put them in her safe, she, thinking it would help the Judge to have the lists in the safe when and if he came by her office late, much later after his dinner engagement, determined that she would.

So, Megan, before midnight, did go to her office, got the faxed lists and, to her surprise, the Judge must have been there earlier, maybe only minutes before, and the single name of one man was already written by the Judge and was in the safe along with the three faxes.

After Megan left, not only did the Judge return after midnight, but in the company of "Win," who, with a gun, forced the Judge to open Megan's safe. The second the safe was opened and "Win" had the three lists and the single name of the winner on a blank piece of paper, he put two bullets into the back of Judge Brooks' head. "Win"'s plan was to take the lists and winner's name with him so that he alone would not only reap the rewards of the three lists, but also go to the Baltimore Trust Company in Bethany Beach the next day and withdraw the million for himself.

When "Win" left the Federal Building that night, the Judge dead in Megan's office, a "dark figure" intercepted and quickly approached "Win" and pumped several rounds into his robust belly. The weapon used had a silencer and so the dull thuds of the bullets were not heard. Then, with dispatch, the "dark figure" removed the papers from "Win"'s pocket: the three lists and the single sheet of paper with one name written on it.

Later that day, the four sheets of paper were in the hands of Roscoe Manley, and thence, into those of Senator Hudson Blake.

"Win"'s body was found and identified early on the morning of October 1. It wasn't until later that morning that Megan found the Judge, dead in her office.

In the Wilmington police reports, they had no suspects or clues in Agar's murder. They knew that the killer of "Win" was probably a "pro" and had no leads or witnesses as to the whereabouts of the assailant.

That morning, October 1, when the Wilmington Police responded to the Federal Building's security guard's call to 911, the Judge was dead, with a gun at his side and, while it bore no fingerprints, was registered to Jamie Agar.

Megan was treated at the scene that morning by a local doctor, who pronounced her "fine" after a fainting spell, only a bruised knee and arm, and she remained in the Judge's private suite while the investigation of the Judge's murder continued in her office.

Delaware State Police questioned Jamie Agar at her home north of Bethany Beach and she had an unshakeable alibi: Roger Thomas, Clay Stevenson and Travis Goodson were all questioned at their respective beach houses in Middlesex Beach and attested to the fact that each had seen, talked with Jamie and had given her their lists before midnight on September 30.

Juan, the houseboy, confirmed that Jamie had not left the Agar home on the night of September 30 nor at any time on October 1.

Unbeknown to everyone in the cases of the murders of "Win" Agar and Judge Sumner Brooks, Sr., the Justice Department in Washington, D.C. had, some months earlier, ordered the Federal Bureau of Investigation to monitor the "political" relationship between Senator Hudson Blake of Nevada and Winfield "Win" Randolph Agar. Their meetings in the Hart Senate Office Building were not only known by the FBI, but their conversations had been taped.

In the end, when the allegations of the FBI and the Delaware State Police and the Wilmington Police were confirmed, the following became very clear: "Win" Agar had taken his wife's small .32 caliber pistol from the night table in the Agar bedroom at the Agar home near Bethany Beach and used it, wearing gloves, to kill Judge Sumner Brooks, Sr. and left the gun to incriminate his wife, whom he discovered, through Robert, his limo driver, that Jamie might have been seeing Clay Stevenson. This was "Win"'s revenge on her; also, the "dark figure," still unknown or located and who might never be, was hired by Senator Blake to kill "Win" and cut him out of the anticipated windfall of millions of dollars to be earned upon the utilization of the three lists developed by Clay Stevenson, Roger Thomas and Travis Goodson; and, lastly, the United States Senate, through their own committee investigations, found Senator Blake guilty as charged by the FBI and the Justice Department, and, when the lists taken from "Win"'s body were found in Senator Blake's secret office safe some weeks later, his peers expelled him from the United States Senate and the Justice Department pushed their case against him and he was imprisoned for life.

At a special hearing, called during the first week in October after the murders of "Win" and the Judge, at the Federal Building in Wilmington, Delaware, all of the principals involved were in attendance, save "Win", the Senator and the Judge.

"What we would all like to know, Your Honor," asked Jamie Agar, "is who won the million dollars my late husband agreed to pay from his Baltimore Trust Company special account in Bethany Beach?"

"The Court, Ma'am, has absolutely no way of knowing. The three lists and the name of the winner on a single sheet of paper that were placed by Megan Greenfield into her safe, were never found."

"Your Honor," Megan said. While nervous, her voice was steady.

"Yes, Miss Greening."

"I know who won the million dollars and I also have the three lists submitted by Messrs. Stevenson, Thomas and Goodson."

There was an audible gasp among the small crowd in the courtroom. Heads turned to get a view of Megan Greening.

"How can that be, Miss Greening?" he asked incredulously.

"I made Xerox copies of the three lists and the single sheet of paper and, on the night of September 30, before midnight, I put them in my center desk drawer before I left the office. I know, Your Honor, that I betrayed a trust of my beloved Judge Brooks, but he had instructed me to make a file and I intended to put those copies in it, as a matter of record, at a later date. Here are the four sheets of paper, Your Honor."

A court clerk received the papers from Miss Greening and handed them to the presiding judge.

"Well, Ladies and Gentlemen, I have the four sheets of paper in my hands. Three are copies of the original faxes received in Miss Greening's office on the night of September 30, just these few days ago, from the Agar home near Bethany Beach and were from Mr. Clay Stevenson, Mr. Roger Thomas and Mr.

Travis Goodson. The fourth is a copy of a single sheet, in Judge Brooks' handwriting, with a single name: *ROGER THOMAS*."

* * * *

Dr. Roger Thomas pledged $500,000 as a matching fund with Johns Hopkins University Hospital to focus immediate medical research on the bipolar illness. Dr. Thomas would serve as the Director of the project, named BI-CURE.

* * * *

Travis and Ainsley Goodson signed a $4 million contract with a publisher in New York City to write a book about surviving a plane crash and escaping as hostages of rebels in Nicaragua.

* * * *

Jamie Agar, widow, deeded the Agar beach house to Bethany Beach as a summer home for needy young girls and boys from the Sussex County area of southern Delaware. A substantial fund was provided

to maintain the home and pay all expenses of the
children for transportation and all medical treatment required. The large house was staffed by a
dozen employees. They prepared all meals and provided professional supervision of the children at a
new swimming pool and wading pool built on the
property, as well as a new, large playground near the
putting green. Further, Mrs. Agar provided ten com-
puters and trained instructors for the groups that
stayed at the home for two-week periods and had the
whole system connected to the Internet for educational development and promotion.

Jamie Agar bought a seven-bedroom penthouse
overlooking Central Park in New York City.

* * * *

Clay Stevenson was appointed by the President
as the United States Ambassador to the United Nations. Upon his unanimous confirmation by the
United States Senate, and sworn in by the President
of the United States in the Oval Office at the White
House, he began to court Jamie Agar. At first he
called for her in his U.N. limousine for official functions. But, very soon, he drove his own new Fleetwood Cadillac, on private business, after he and
Jamie were wed.

BOOKS BY WADE B. FLEETWOOD

THE GHOST ON ERRETT ROAD
MURDER ON THE BOARDWALK
MURDER ON THE OCEAN CITY PIER
MURDER AT THE HENLOPEN INN
MURDER IN THE FENWICK ISLAND
LIGHTHOUSE
MURDER IN OCEAN PINES
MURDER ON THE DeBRAAK
MURDER ON ASSATEAGUE ISLAND
HMS DeBRAAK: LAST VOYAGE, 1798
ADAM IN DELAWARE
MURDER IN BETHANY BEACH
MURDER AT THE CONVENTION CENTER
MURDER IN REHOBOTH BEACH
THE CASE OF THE PELICAN'S FEATHER
A BEACH REUNION IN FALLS CHURCH,
VIRGINIA
THE QUEST

About The Author

-Born in Baker, Oregon, November 3, 1924;

-Attended public schools in Oregon and Boise, Idaho, graduating from Boise High School in 1942;

-Attended Boise Junior College, 1942-43, now Boise State University;

-Graduated from the University of Idaho, Moscow, Idaho, 1947, with a B.A. degree in Political Science;

-A secondary teacher of history and debate for five years in Boise and Miami, Florida;

-Married Betty Spencer of Nampa, Idaho, 1948;

-On the U.S. Capitol Police Force, 1949-1953, and attended night school at Georgetown University in Washington, D.C., where he earned a Master of Arts degree in Political Science, 1955;

-Won a Ford Foundation Scholarship to undertake a history project at the University of California in Berkeley, California, at the Bancroft Library, 1955-56;

-Director, Idaho State Headquarters, on the small, core team of friends, when the late Senator Frank Church first won election to the U.S. Senate. Fleetwood served as his Executive Secretary, 1957-1963, in Washington, D.C. They had been friends since ten years of age and grew up in the same block in Boise;

-A Public Information Officer, Agency for International Development, Latin American Bureau, and The Office of Public Affairs, 1963-1983, when he retired from 30 years of Federal Government Service;

-Coastal newspaper columnist for a number of years when he began writing murder mystery novels, "The Quest" being his sixteenth. All outsold national bestsellers in the Mid-Atlantic coastal resort towns by a ratio of two to one, 1984-92;

-He is a past member of the National Press Club, Washington, D.C., and was a founder of Washington Independent Writers;

-Currently, Fleetwood is a member of the University of Idaho Alumni Association, the Nation's Capital Chapter; the Georgetown University Alumni Club of Washington, D.C.; Patron, Concerts at the Beach, CURI, Inc., Washington, D.C.; Boise State University Alumni Association; Patron, Friends of the South Coastal Library Inc., Bethany Beach, Delaware; an active partner of the Carter Center, Atlanta, Georgia; on the Regent's Club, the Martin Peace Institute Endowment, the University of Idaho Foundation, Moscow, Idaho; and a supporter of many charitable organizations, both local and national.

An Order Form

If you want a copy of "A Beach Reunion in Falls Church, Virginia," I'll be happy to autograph and personalize a book for you at $10, including mailing, while the supply lasts. At the same cost, copies of "The Case of the Pelican's Feather" are still available. A limited number of other back titles are also on hand, including "Murder on the Boardwalk," "Murder on the Ocean City Pier," "Murder at the Convention Center," and, at $15, "The Ghost on Errett Road."

I am enclosing $_____ for

_____

_____

_____

Send this form to: Wade B. Fleetwood
439 Hampton Court
Falls Church, Virginia 22046